UNTALENTED

Katrina Archer

ganache
media

A Ganache Media Book
Vancouver

2014 Ganache Media Commonwealth print edition

ISBN 978-0-9880512-4-9

Cover design by Heather McDougal

Maps by Katrina Archer and Heather McDougal

www.ganachemedia.com

For Grand-mère

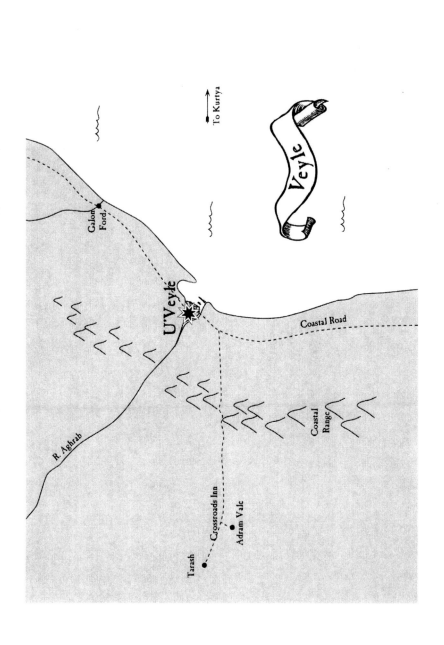

UNTALENTED

CHAPTER 1

"Untalented."

One little word. How could one little word sound so big? So huge there was no getting around it?

"But ..." Saroya cast about for something—anything!—that might change the verdict.

"There are no 'buts'," Doyenne Ganarra said. Her stern, lined face brooked no argument. "Three Tests. That's all anyone gets. Your results are consistent, at least." The doyenne handed back Saroya's test slate and chalk. Saroya took them with the same enthusiasm she would a live, venomous snake. "Within the month," the doyenne continued, "you will gather your possessions and leave the cloister. Perhaps the mines will take you."

Saroya caught a fleeting glance of pity on the other examiner's face before both Adepts swept from the room. She looked around but there was nothing lying in reach to throw at Doyenne Ganarra's retreating head—but who was she kidding? As if she'd ever work up that much courage. A glint of gilt thread on the woman's headdress winked back, taunting her.

Drained, Saroya leaned against the window. The Testing seemed to go so well! Instead—*Untalented. Too scattered* ... The stone of the frame cooled her temple. The sun shone outside, but the cheeriness outdoors eluded her. She wished the two happy, chattering students crossing the courtyard would shut up. Couldn't they tell her world had just ended? Her hand shaking, Saroya worried at a strand of copper hair.

Leave! Saroya tallied up in her head what little money she'd saved. Not enough for getting by even in tiny Adram Vale. No guild would take her now, not without a certificate of Talent with the seal of the Order of Adepts. Even if she evaded hard labour in the mines and found other work, it would take months to earn enough on a servant or field hand's stipend to leave the village. What would she do in a town full of strangers? Better strangers, though, than a tiny village where everybody knew just what she was.

Untalented. Saroya shuddered.

∞ ∞

The healer led Isolte into the queen's inner room. Isolte wrinkled her nose. The air was close and smelled of stale sheets, perspiration, and healing herbs.

Isolte stiffened. Queen Padvai's once shining auburn hair clung in lank tendrils to her forehead. Her eyes glittered with fever. Beads of moisture formed on her nose, cheeks, and forehead. The gauntness of her face left no doubt that this was no simple spring cold. Padvai lay in the rumpled bed, fighting for her life.

Isolte brushed past the Healer and leaned over the bed. Padvai's eyes zagged back and forth, unseeing. She laboured to breathe.

"Padvai," Isolte said. "Sister. I am here."

Padvai's gaze locked onto Isolte's, and she clutched her sister's hand. "Isolte? Where's Dhilain? I asked for Dhilain ..."

Isolte sniffed. Why must she always play second fiddle to brother dearest?

"Isolte. The child. You must tell the family about the child."

Isolte drew back, startled, but Padvai's grip was stronger than she would have guessed.

"What child?" Was there something she was forgetting? Isolte wracked her brain.

"The Adepts. In the vale. Adram Vale."

"Padvai, you're confused. If you sleep, it will all be better in the morning."

"No." Her sister's breathing grew shallower. She squeezed Isolte's fingers harder. "Not confused. In Adram Vale." She paused, hoarse. "*Our* child."

Isolte gasped, and glanced at the healer. Had he overheard? No.

Padvai pleaded with her. "Promise me. Tell Dhilain. But —" A fit of coughing seized her. "Urdig. Urdig must not know."

"Of course." Isolte patted Padvai's hand, hoping to soothe her and get her own hand back. "A child, Padvai. Such interesting news. Was that all you wished to tell me?" Doubt crept into Padvai's face. "No more sins to confess while we are about it? The identity of King Urdig's cuckold, perhaps?"

Padvai moaned. The healer rushed to the bed and shooed Isolte away. "That's enough for now. You may visit again tomorrow if you wish."

Isolte acquiesced. She was coming away with more than she'd expected, anyway. "Good night, sister. Sweet dreams."

One could be civil in one's little victories, after all.

∞ ∞

Life had been easy before the Testing sealed her fate, but the next morning Saroya got a taste of things to come. Entering her builder's class, she dropped her slate on her desk. The other students filing in avoided looking at her.

The Adept teacher handed back the granary design grades. Saroya was especially pleased with her idea for keeping out vermin. Rats could only jump so high. She'd clad the base of every wall and beam in her mockup with flattened iron pilfered from the smithy. The slippery metal foiled the rats' grip on wood. Saroya frowned down at her paper. There must be some mistake! She approached the Adept after class.

"Beg pardon, but I think you forgot to grade my granary

design," Saroya said, careful to keep her tone polite.

Seated at his desk, he still managed to look down his nose at her. "Not worth my time—grading the papers of a student not moving on to the Builder's Guild."

"But—" She was saying that an awful lot, lately.

He cut her off. "You will no longer hand in assignments, and you will remain quiet during the lesson. Ingrate—you're lucky I even let you stay in class." He turned back to his papers, dismissing her.

She froze in disbelief. Her cheeks burned—a freshman student arriving for the introductory class had heard every word. She hurried from the room.

Saroya ducked her head whenever she saw an Adept, flinching at the sight of their silvery grey robes, a constant reminder of her new non-status. In class after class, it was the same: she had ceased to exist for the Adepts. Why waste teaching time on an Untalent, someone who'd never master a vocation?

With her so-called friends, it was even worse. When Saroya sat down in the refectory at midday, Martezha elbowed her in the back as she passed by with her own bowl of noodles with mutton.

"Aren't they giving you the boot? You should be serving us dinner instead of sitting here."

Saroya put her knife down and stared into her lap. Steam wafted up from the food, adding heat to the shame burning her cheeks. Blast Martezha! *Like I don't already know I'm useless.*

"I take it back. Don't you clean the doyenne's chamber

pots now? Nobody wants someone that filthy near food."
Martezha flounced away, secure in her singing Talent.

Out of the corner of her eye, Saroya sensed a presence
next to her, and a plate slid into view on the table beside her.
She looked up as her roommate Nalini Ferlen sat down.

"You don't have to do this, you know," Saroya said.

"We always sit together." Nalini dug with relish into her
pasta. She grinned around her spoon. "Besides, you know
how much I love sticking it to Martezha and her friends. So
she's a Singer. She should be resting her voice instead of
gossiping all the time."

Saroya smiled. "I've never understood how you manage
to fit all that food into you." Nalini's slim frame bordered on
waiflike.

"That's the spirit. Change the subject. Always lifts my
mood. Look, it seems awful now, but you'll figure something
out. I can help you get organized with the council."

"The council … Do you know where they send people
like me? The mines." Saroya's chest tightened at the mere
thought of the mines—living underground, never seeing the
sun, choking on ore dust. But Doyenne Ganarra had ordered
her to report to the village council. They would not give her
a choice.

"Better that than the brothels."

"What do you know about it?" Saroya rounded on her
friend. "You're guild-bound, normal, just like everyone else
except me. You'll never have to worry about where your next
meal is coming from." Nalini could not look her in the eye.

Saroya tossed her spoon down onto her plate, spilling noodles onto the table. Conversations died at the tables surrounding them. "You know what will happen to me. Pretty soon you won't want to be seen with me. I mean it— if it's going to make things hard for you, go sit somewhere else." More than anything, she wanted Nalini to stay. But not at the cost of always seeing pity in her friend's eyes.

"I'm still your friend," Nalini said. "But I don't sit with sulkers. The trick is to act like you don't mind. If you look all mopey and act like the barn dog, people will treat you like the barn dog."

∞ ∽

The sun shone and a light ocean breeze played in the flags when Padvai of House Roshan, Queen of Veyle, was laid to rest. The gathered nobility stood in their mourning finery, sober as King Urdig delivered the eulogy.

Isolte whispered in her husband Loric's ear. "Do you think he will take another wife?"

Loric glanced at her in irritation. "He needs an heir, Isolte. Of course he will remarry." His tone turned biting. "But you need not worry it will be you. He'll look for some bright young thing, with child-bearing hips."

Isolte pursed her lips. "And leave you, Loric? I had my chance for Urdig's hand long ago."

Loric arched an eyebrow, but Isolte continued. "I'm not certain he needs an heir. He might already have one. Unless Padvai whelped a bastard."

Loric stifled a startled laugh. "Aren't we just full of secrets today? My, my."

Isolte gave him a knowing simper. "Why Loric, if we don't find some way of getting you onto the throne of Veyle soon, I'll never be queen."

Loric schooled his features as he turned back to watch Urdig throw the first handfuls of soil into his wife's grave. It was a good day to be alive, Loric mused as he catalogued the damage he could do with the secrets Urdig had failed to bury with Padvai.

∽ ∽

The council building, of large timbers and stone, was wedged between a merchant's shop and an inn on the north side of the Adram Vale village square. It did triple-duty as meeting hall, post station, and tax office for the village. Saroya took a deep calming breath and went through the door. Inside, her eyes adjusted to the lack of sunlight. A large woman glanced up from an untidy pile of parchment.

"Yes? Do I know you?" the woman asked.

"N—" Saroya cleared her throat. "No. I'm from the Cloister."

"Oh. One of those." Disinterested, the woman turned back to sorting her parchments.

Saroya walked up to her and held out her letter. "One of those?"

"The Cloister only sends but one kind of person to see the council."

"Doyenne Ganarra told me to give this to the head councilman." Saroya held out the letter with the Cloister's seal.

The woman snatched the rolled up paper from Saroya and waved her away. "He's out. Wait over there." She indicated a stool in the corner.

Saroya's mouth tightened but, with a single longing look at the padded chair in the other corner, she took a seat on the stool.

For an hour, she waited. And waited. She tapped her foot on the floor, counted the small dimples in the wall missing plaster, played an imaginary game of Queen's Gambit on the tiles of floor. *This is stupid.* She stood up and smoothed out her tunic.

"Excuse me," Saroya said. The papers on the table continued to fly from one messy pile to the next. "I said—"

"I heard you." The woman didn't even glance up.

Saroya sighed. "If you told me where he was, I could find him myself and stop wasting your time."

The woman just pointed at the stool. Saroya ignored her and made for the chair.

"The stool, I said. Learn your place."

Saroya stiffened, but a good retort eluded her. Might as well wait outside in the sunshine.

"Good riddance," the woman threw at her retreating back.

Small thatched houses lined the square. Outside one, a young mother washed her laundry in a vat, her toddlers playing with carved wooden blocks at her feet. Two boys chased a scruffy dog. A large oak tree shaded the middle of the square. Saroya propped herself against the gnarled trunk with a good view of the council house door. She brooded.

Even if she avoided the mines, any other menial job left her at the mercy of her employers. If they took a dislike to her, they would throw her out without a second thought. And scrabbling around in the dark, digging for ore—bile crept up her throat just thinking about it. The Cloister students traded tales of the unfortunates drafted into the mines, how they came out years later pale and scrawny, and died of a racking cough not long after.

On the far side of the square, the two boys now targeted a pile of rags leaning against a retaining wall, pitching stones at the heap and laughing. Saroya paid no mind until the mound moved. An old beggar shook off a tattered blanket, raising a trembling arm to deflect the hail of pebbles. The boys' laughter no longer sounded so innocent to Saroya's ears. The larger boy, emboldened, ran up to the beggar and kicked him.

"We told you to stay away from here, you dirty Untalent."

"Yeah! We know you stole that chicken from Armen. Prob'ly Da's good shirt from the line, too."

Saroya shot to her feet. "Hey! Leave him alone!"

The stocky boy sneered at her then scampered off, followed by his friend. Saroya stared at the beggar, seeing not a withered old man, but her future. What kind of life was that?

A small seed of sympathy and rebellion blossomed in Saroya's heart. It wasn't fair that a simple test could ruin so many lives. It wasn't fair that the guilds controlled all the good work. She didn't feel any different today than she had before the Testing, but now she was supposed to believe she was worthless? After years of praise from her teachers? Saroya kicked at a pebble. Why?

Just last week, Nalini had popped the bread Saroya baked into her mouth and exclaimed, "This is delicious! What did you do to the crust?"

"Remember how Adept Perga showed us the difference between steaming and boiling vegetables? It gave me an idea about dry heat versus wet heat. So I put a pan of water in the oven with the bread."

And it had turned out great. Adept Perga even went back for seconds, saying through a mouthful, "You have a bright future as a baker." Except now, the Chef's Guild would never let her in, mouth-watering recipes or not. All for lack of that blasted certificate of Talent.

"*A cluttered mind will lead you astray. Only a studious mind finds its one true path,*" Saroya mimicked the doyenne's didactic tone. "I did study, blast it!" And it got her exactly nowhere. No path had presented itself. At least, no path she cared to tread.

A man coming into the square from the east road distracted her, and the beggar scuttled away. The new arrival sauntered towards the council house and went inside. Saroya walked up to a small girl playing with a wooden ball.

"Hi."

The girl rolled the ball shyly.

"That man who just went into the council house. Was that Councilman Reeth?"

A nod. Saroya took a hard candy out of her pocket and gave it to the girl, who popped it in her mouth before grinning and scampering away.

Saroya approached the door of the council house, but, reaching for the handle, she paused. Her fingers hovered over the iron latch. The unvarnished wood loomed before her like the gate of a prison.

Deliberately, she turned back to the square. She'd find something else to do. Something she chose for herself.

∞ ∽

The intruder padded around the room in the fading light. A foolish risk he now regretted, but when the opportunity presented to sneak into the cloister dormitories, he couldn't resist. If he returned empty-handed, His Lordship would express his displeasure in unsavoury ways.

The six previous rooms had yielded no results. He'd just avoided being caught by a group of chattering girls, ducking into a closet before they rounded the corner. He needed to find something soon.

He rifled through the items on the night table, his frustration mounting. He rubbed the prickly growth of beard on his cheeks, mulling over his options. One more room—he'd search one more then leave off. Bad enough if he didn't deliver, but if anybody discovered him, he didn't want to imagine what His Lordship would do in his ire. "Don't be seen … no inns, camp in the woods." He cursed the need for secrecy, and scratched at the spider bite on his hip. Woods indeed. There was something to be said for a good mug of ale in the comfort of a tavern.

He'd almost given up when his search bore fruit. He held the object up to the last rays of the sun filtering through the window, and smiled. Good thing he could read. Then again, His Lordship wouldn't have chosen him for this mission otherwise. He backed out of the room, double-checking that he'd left its contents as he'd found them. "Take nothing." His orders had been clear. Everything looked neat and tidy. Undisturbed. No one would notice he'd been here. He scurried toward the back stairs, already tasting the beer he'd treat himself to with his fee. The creak of shoe on wood at the landing down the hall caused him to glance back. He glimpsed golden hair as someone entered the hallway. He hastened his escape.

CHAPTER 2

Long after sunset, Saroya hopped off the cart at the head of the track that led back to the Cloister. She thanked the farmer for his time before the wagon lumbered off, the mule eager for dinner. Saroya knew she'd missed hers.

She stopped as she rounded a curve and the lights of the Cloister came into view. The warm glow from the windows reminded her how little time remained to her here. The only home she'd ever known—in less than a month, the Adepts would cast her out.

She approached the door to the room she shared with Nalini, but something felt off. The door was cracked open and the room dark—Nalini still off somewhere for the evening. Probably the library. Saroya smiled. Nalini, guaranteed a spot in the Healer's Guild at year end, still wasn't taking any chances. She studied at every opportunity.

Saroya pushed open the door and groped for the nightstand, already rummaging in her pouch for her flint to light the candle. She stubbed her toe on something lying on the floor, stumbled and tripped. "Blast it, Nalini, can't you stack your books more carefully?" Now she'd have a nice bruise on her shin. Her toe throbbed. She felt her way more carefully to the candle. She lit the taper and tossed her pouch on the bed, turning to get a good look at the room. And cursed again.

This was beyond untidy. Nalini's side of the room looked reasonable but a herd of unruly pigs might have rampaged around Saroya's side. The door to her clothes cabinet hung open, clothing strewn everywhere. What a mess!—books scattered willy-nilly and the small pottery vase she'd made at age twelve smashed in pieces on the floor. And there, scrawled in black paint on the wall above the bed: the word "Useless".

Saroya swallowed. She spotted the wooden box in which she kept her few personal treasures dumped upside down next to her desk chair. She nudged a pillow out of her way and bent to right the box. Nothing tumbled out before the lid clapped down again. Her hand trembled as she opened it.

Gone. Everything was gone. The silver ring, her only real piece of jewelry. The bead necklace Nalini made for her fourteenth birthday. The small stash of coins she'd saved from the meagre allowance the Adepts gave her. The eagle feather she'd found three years ago. Even the apple blossom she'd pressed flat when Juren put it in her hair before kissing her on her fifteenth birthday.

She slumped against the chair. The feather was just a

sentimental keepsake, but she'd been counting on the money to helped establish herself outside the Cloister. And the ring, the ring! Shoshana Adept showed it to her when she was a young child and let her hold it. "It came from your mother, dear." Silver with a blue stone, a delicate knot-like pattern etched its circumference. On her twelfth birthday, Shoshana Adept placed it in Saroya's palm and closed her fingers around it. "You're old enough to keep it yourself now." Saroya's jaw tightened—she'd lost a link to her family. She gritted her teeth. No. Someone stole it.

She collected herself and pressed her fingers against the bottom of the box, feeling for the hidden catch. With a soft thunk, a small latch released and the base came out to reveal a hidden tray. Saroya sighed with relief. She muttered a thank you to the Cloister carpenter who'd built the box as a gift for a lonely little girl.

She brushed her fingers across the piece of parchment that nestled in the compartment. She didn't lift it out. It was old, and crumbling; she didn't want to risk damaging it, though she could never forget the words written on it.

Always know you are loved and missed.

When you are ready, search for Veshwa. Loyal servant of Veyle, she will tell you who you are.

The short letter always left her with mixed feelings. Someone claimed to love her. Then why did they abandon her here? And how was she ever supposed to find this Veshwa? She'd asked around in Adram Vale, but no one had ever heard of such a person. "When you are ready ..."

Ready. What a laugh. Saroya snorted. "Guess now's as good a time to start looking as any," Saroya muttered to herself. "It's not like I have any better prospects." She'd always hoped to surprise her long-lost family, the prodigal daughter returning with a lengthy list of accomplishments under her belt. Now? Maybe Veshwa could help her find work. Then again, she—he?—might be less than happy to find an Untalent on the doorstep. The cryptic note frustrated her, but it was all she had of her family now.

Saroya replaced the base, closed the box, and put it back underneath her bed. She set about righting the mess of her belongings. Hanging a tunic back in the dresser, she heard a floorboard creak, then a gasp.

Nalini stood in the doorway. "What happened here?"

"Someone's been through my things. It's all right—they left yours alone."

"Oh, Saroya, I'm so sorry. We should report this to the doyenne."

"There's no point. They're long gone."

Nalini frowned. "Someone in the hall might have seen the person come out. I'm going to find an Adept." She hurried away.

Saroya decided it wouldn't hurt to at least put away her clothes while waiting. She got them all packed away again, and the bed remade, by the time Nalini returned—alone, and looking angry.

"So?" Saroya asked.

"Ermina Adept said she could do nothing for someone

silly enough to leave valuables unlocked in their room."
Nalini frowned. "I did run into Tarmi—he said he thought
he saw a stranger leaving the dorm."

"If that's true, we'll never find my stuff."

"Look at your lute! Why would anybody do something
like that?"

The lute she'd never learned to play properly leaned in
splinters against her desk, a broken string curled against its
neck. Saroya turned her head to hide her incipient tears.
"Maybe they did me a favour. Now I don't have to pick and
choose what to bring with me when I leave."

Nalini looked at the wall with distaste. "I'll scrub that for
you. It makes me so angry just looking at it." She pulled a
package wrapped in cloth from her waist pouch. "Here, I
figured you'd miss supper. It's not much."

Saroya's stomach gurgled. She unwrapped the cloth to
find a couple of slices of bread and cold meat, with a raw
carrot adding a splash of colour. "You're the best." She
tucked into the food.

"How did it go with the village council?"

Saroya chewed her food, buying time. Nalini raised an
eyebrow. Saroya sighed.

"I didn't see the head councilman," Saroya said.

"Why the blazes not?"

"This horrible woman ... She was just awful."

"Because you're ...?"

"You can't even say it. Say the blasted word!"

"Fine. Untalented. The council was your best chance,

Saroya. You should go back tomorrow."

"No. I'd rather go somewhere nobody knows me and see what happens. Maybe someone in Tarash will take me on as a healer's assistant."

"But … you're not Talented enough—" Nalini bit her lip.

"I might not know as much about healing as you do but I know enough to help people."

"The things you don't know could kill people."

"Thanks for backing me up."

"I'm just telling you the truth." Nalini's worried expression told her just what her friend thought of her plan.

Saroya shrugged, and fingered one of the lute's snapped strings. "I'll be fine."

If she said it often enough, she'd start to believe it.

∞ ∞

Loric tossed his gloves onto Isolte's dressing table as he strode past it to the window. Fine as the view of his estate was, he would not be satisfied until his vista opened onto the palace grounds of U'Veyle. He spun around and scowled at his wife.

"My man just returned from Adram Vale," Loric said.

"And?"

"Several children were abandoned at the Cloister."

"A pity he could not find out more." Loric couldn't resist an enigmatic smile. Isolte's eyes widened. "You're hiding something!"

"There is a child—a girl. My man found a trinket—one

inferring close ties to House Roshan, and thus Padvai. As instructed, he left it there." Loric held out a rubbing to Isolte. She stared at the inscription. It did mention her maiden House.

Isolte frowned. "Even a bastard won't force King Urdig to abdicate. He's too popular."

"Ah, but if we can shake the Houses' confidence in his line …"

"That's not so easily done, Loric."

"It is if the child is Untalented."

Isolte gasped. Loric continued.

"Anything implicating Padvai also taints House Roshan's line, unfortunately for you, my dear." He paced in front of the fireplace, tapping a cheek with his forefinger.

Isolte lowered her eyes. Loric blamed her for their son's failure at his first Testing. There was no other explanation, now that the stain of Untalent had shown itself in her family through her sister's child. He saw her bite back the first retort that came to her lips. Good. Baiting him with his own mistake all those years ago would not serve her cause.

Isolte brushed an imagined crumb from her silks. "Better to get rid of her."

"So mercenary, Isolte."

"We need not kill her. Pack her off into indenture somewhere, maybe send her across the ocean to Kurtya."

"People have a nasty way of popping back onto the scene when you least want them to."

"But if she dies, Urdig has no heir."

"Urdig could live for years—years! I have no intention of waiting that long. We need a scandal—soon. To begin with, we will not breathe a word of a child." Isolte cocked up a questioning eyebrow. "Go to Urdig. Tell him ... Say you are concerned about your sister's legacy." Loric paced back and forth, growing more excited. "Convince him to establish a trust for training students in their Guilds. In her memory. Her interest in the poor, their education ..."

"And we know just the young people to suggest." Isolte clapped her hands.

"And when they arrive, we'll have a little surprise for everyone."

∽ ∾

Saroya frowned at the dust cloud on the road far below. The quiet and the view from her secret spot on an outcrop sometimes helped her think, and she needed a bright idea now that she'd spurned the local village council. The cloister and its outbuildings lay small in the valley, the early spring growth on the trees lining its slopes bright green. Burnt sienna roof tiles shimmered beneath a heat haze.

The day fast approached when the Adepts would force her to fend for herself and she still had no idea where to start. She had just ruled out working on one of the neighbouring farms when the disturbance on the valley road caught her eye. A farmer heading back home from trading his early spring vegetables with the Adepts stopped his mule team and moved them to the side of the road. Horsemen!

The distance hid any identifying characteristics. With a last glance for the party on the road, Saroya pelted back down her short cut through the olive orchard. While the Adepts stayed close-mouthed about their business with visitors, Saroya was an expert at gleaning good gossip from the servants, especially now that they seemed to think she'd joined their ranks.

Saroya dashed into the stable yard, out of breath from the run down the hill. Trotting past the stables, she picked several burrs out of her tunic, hoping to catch a glimpse of the visitors in the courtyard.

"Saroya!"

"Sorry, Durin! Gotta run … I saw horsemen coming up the valley road. Maybe I can catch them before they get to the gates," she threw back over her shoulder.

"Too late." The head stableman's answer stopped her in her tracks. "Doyenne's already greeted them. Moved on to her study ten minutes ago. Come see the horses."

Who knew how long they'd be before they announced any news? She turned and headed for the stable door.

"Don't see beauties like these too often round these parts." Durin stared appreciatively into the stable corridor. Saroya peered in. She had to agree. With a horse tethered in front of each of four empty stalls, stablehands removed gleaming leather saddles, or scraped lather off heaving flanks. The biggest horse Saroya had ever seen, a gorgeous black, was already being taken to a corral for a warmdown. The others, similarly spirited animals, gave the Adepts' handlers a hard time, stamping and prancing from side to side. If the curve of their necks and grace of their steps hadn't been enough, the tack told her these must be noblemen's steeds. Worked silver adorned the bridles, bits clinking as a stableboy hung them from a peg. The burnished leather even smelled richer than usual. She turned to Durin.

"Do you know who they are?" she asked.

"Didn't notice any standards or crests."

"And they didn't say anything about why they were here?"

Durin grinned at her. "Nope. Could be they're just passing through and Crossroads Inn isn't good enough for them. Took about as much notice of old Durin as of a fly on the wall. Have to talk to the doyenne if you want to know more."

Saroya smiled ruefully back at him. "We both know how likely the doyenne is to tell *me* anything."

"Speaking of Doyenne Ganarra, asked me to talk to you, she did. Knows you like the horses. Might want to consider helping us around the stables when term ends. Not a bad life —easy to teach you how to train 'em, you've already got a nice seat and hands on the reins." Durin rubbed his chin. "Won't be able to get you involved in full breeding and husbandry, now, 'coz the Agriculture Guild would string me up, but I can always use an extra set of hands. Pay's not great, but better'n nothing. Don't hold no truck with them that says someone like you's bad luck."

The prospect of mucking out stalls for the rest of her life smelled as good as the manure she'd be shovelling, but Saroya didn't want to offend Durin.

"Can I think about it and let you know later?" Durin nodded. "I'd better run. Maybe the visitors will be at dinner. Thanks for letting me see the horses!" She raced off towards her dormitory.

She came flying off the second floor landing, already planning how to break her news to Nalini. Visitors were gossip fodder, but noblemen! She burst into her room, the door slamming into the wall behind her.

"Nalini, wait 'til you hear—"

"Saroya, where have you been!" Nalini interrupted. "There are king's men here and the doyenne's ordered everyone to the Great Hall by third bell. I'm late as it is and you're not even changed! Look at you—nettles in your hair, and the mud!—you can't expect to be allowed into the Great Hall with your tunic like that."

Saroya gaped at her and closed her mouth with a click. So much for being the first with news. She headed for the mirror they shared to take stock. Blast Nalini for being right. Saroya rubbed at a smudge griming her freckles. She could do nothing about the grass-stained tunic.

"I think I have a clean tunic in the chest. Can you dig it out for me while I wash up?"

Saroya tugged her filthy clothes over her head. She scrubbed her face and then plucked at her tangled hair. By the time Nalini found the clean outfit and tossed it to her, she was somewhat presentable. She twirled around for inspection.

"You're fine, let's go!" Nalini said.

Tugging on her sandals, Saroya winced at her dirt-caked toes. Nobody would look at her feet, right? She and Nalini hurried out the door towards the Great Hall in the main building.

A hundred voices whispering rustled underneath the roof timbers of the Great Hall. Nalini and Saroya wedged themselves into the crowd to the left of the doors, close to the front of the hall. They peered over the heads of the other students at the raised dais. Several Adepts already sat to the left of the lectern.

Conversation in the hall died down as Doyenne Ganarra entered. She wore flowing robes of grey, her hair swept back underneath the official mark of her rank, a rounded gold-embroidered headdress. Five men followed her in. Their long-legged, confident stride contrasted with her smooth, graceful progress. The doyenne reached the lectern, the men taking up positions standing to her right. They wore travel clothes, sturdy leggings, and long dust cloaks. They bore no identifiable House sigils. Each man carried a long sword belted to his waist. Two had quivers with arrows strapped across their shoulders.

The doyenne cleared her throat before she spoke. Her mellow voice carried surprisingly well to the far corners of the hall.

"Adepts and students, please join me in welcoming these

weary travellers as our guests. They have journeyed all the way from U'Veyle with a request from the king himself."

An excited murmur ran through the hall. What could the king want with a ragtag group of orphans and students? It must be something to do with the Adepts. Nalini gave her a puzzled glance. Saroya shrugged as Doyenne Ganarra continued.

"To honour the memory of Queen Padvai, King Urdig wishes to make several gifts to the people of the realm. The queen believed in educating those less fortunate, and as recognition of the work of the Adepts here in Adram Vale, he offers those of you who will be leaving us this year the opportunity for higher learning in the capital. Not the provincial capital, Tarash, but U'Veyle itself. Those of you graduating in the spring will instead leave us tomorrow." She turned to the men standing beside her on the platform. "These men are members of the King's Guards, and will escort you on the journey to U'Veyle."

A stunned silence greeted her words. Saroya felt Nalini grip her arm hard, but she was too focused on the doyenne to spare her a look.

"After dinner, the following students shall return to their rooms to pack up those belongings they wish to take to the capital: Tarmi Ageda, Martezha Baghore, Nalini Ferlen ..." All told, twenty-one students would be making the journey. But not Saroya. "King Urdig honours us by giving you this most precious of opportunities. Justify our confidence in your abilities by excelling in all your endeavours. Now, our guests will join us in the dining hall for the evening meal. Please make them welcome."

The Great Hall began to empty, and Nalini turned to Saroya, her face stricken. Saroya struggled to hide her disappointment. She could tell from her friend's expression, fast turning to pity, that she hadn't succeeded. "It's all right, Nalini. You and I both know there is no guild for me in the capital." Her voice caught as she continued. "Let's go. We're missing dinner."

Saroya picked at her food. As if being passed over for the trip were not humiliation enough, upon their arrival at the dining hall, the Adepts separated the two friends, with Nalini directed to sit at the long banquet table with the others making the journey, the king's men, Doyenne Ganarra, and several higher-ranking Adepts. They forced Saroya to sit with the students one year her junior. She ignored their whispered comments and sidelong glances as she stared at her plate. She could not bring herself to look at the head table. She didn't trust herself not to burst into tears of rage and frustration if she did.

She heard—faintly, as though she stood at the bottom of a chasm—the doyenne toasting the king's men, and the new members of their party. The dumplings on her plate blurred in front of her. She *would not* cry. What she told Nalini was true. There were no guilds for her in the capital, or anywhere. Time to stop dreaming. Opportunity was for the Talented.

Seeing the expression on her face, the boy sitting

opposite her turned away, embarrassed. One of the king's men, likely their leader, stood up and raised his glass to the doyenne. He praised the Cloister and the Adepts' devotion to their charges, but as he described the trip ahead, and the fine schools in the capital, something in Saroya snapped. With shaking hands, she put down her cutlery, shoved back her chair, and hurried between the long tables to the door. She barely noticed heads turning her way, and a pause in the speech. She reached the stairs to the dormitory, and let the sobs escape her.

It wasn't like she'd woken up that morning filled with excitement and high hopes. Yet the loss of something she'd never even had hit her like a punch in the stomach. This was the first of what promised to be endless demonstrations of everything she'd get passed over for from now on.

Saroya managed to compose herself by the time Nalini returned to their room an hour later. She sat on the bed, watching her friend choose what to bring with her in her new life.

"U'Veyle," Nalini was saying. "Even if I did well at the Tarash Healer's Guild I'd be lucky to ever see the capital. We might have been able to see each other if you made it to Tarash, too, but now ..."

Nalini held up two tunics, and Saroya pointed to the one in her left hand. Nalini tossed it onto the growing pile of items on the bed.

"You'd have been more likely to find a good House to engage you in the capital, too."

Saroya sighed. "Nalini, I'm really happy for you. Could we not talk about me any more?" She got off the bed and helped Nalini sort through her clothes. "I can't believe you're leaving tomorrow."

"I know. There's hardly any time to say goodbye. In a way, I wish I was still going to Tarash."

"You can't be serious. You'll learn a lot more apprenticing in U'Veyle than from some country healer in Tarash."

"I know. But U'Veyle's so much closer to Galon Ford."

"How can your parents still be upset about the healer thing?"

Nalini had looked so forlorn when she first arrived at the Cloister five years ago. Her parents, unhappy about her nascent healing Talent, made the long journey from her hometown of Galon Ford only to dump her in Adram Vale. The Ferlen clan excelled at building; the talk of the Cloister revolved for days around the shouting match between Nalini's father and Doyenne Ganarra when the doyenne balked at forcing Nalini into builder's classes. In the end, the doyenne relented; Adram Vale was not renowned for producing strong Talents and the Cloister needed the money. Nalini had been miserable for months.

Nalini handed Saroya a letter. "It came just after your Testing … I didn't want to bother you …" Saroya's eyebrows climbed up her forehead as she read the threat to hold back Nalini's final tuition payment unless Nalini re-Tested as a builder.

"But your parents can't fight your final Testing!"

"Wrong. I'm 'a disgrace to the family line'—the first Ferlen in seven generations who's not a builder."

They heard a quick knock before the door was flung open. An Adept swept into the room, two students carrying a trunk behind her.

"Nalini, everything you wish to take with you to the capital must fit into this trunk." The students set it down with a thunk on the floor. "Anything you need during the ride goes in these saddlebags, but leave room for your daily ration of food. Bring a warm cloak and wear sturdy clothes. The weather could turn at any time. Be ready at dawn tomorrow."

The Adept turned and scowled at Saroya. "You, Saroya, will report to the doyenne's chambers at first light. She was none too pleased with the spectacle you made of yourself in front of our guests." With that, the woman left them as suddenly as she had come.

Saroya exchanged a glum look with her friend, before walking over to the trunk and fingering the latch. The brass hasp felt cold to her touch. She lifted the lid and peered inside. A faint whiff of lavender reached her nostrils. The trunk was lined, with trays at the top for smaller items. It had been used before, its corners scuffed and some of the inner fabric torn. Still, she had never seen anything she wanted more. Suddenly Saroya laughed.

"It's not as if seeing Doyenne Ganarra tomorrow could make me feel any worse," Saroya said. "Do you think she'll give me more laundry chores? Maybe she'll make me clean the chicken coop. Or do a kitchen inventory."

Nalini grinned. "If you don't watch out, she could put you in charge of minding Mistress Jarra." Saroya howled, thinking about having to endure Jarra's endless complaints about her aches and pains, and her constant opining about the deteriorating quality of the current crop of youths.

Saroya and Nalini were still giggling when they finally turned in. Nalini blew out the candle. Saroya tried to sleep but tossed and turned instead. The unfairness of tomorrow —losing both Nalini and her chance at the city, plus facing the doyenne's punishment—kept her awake. Saroya stared at the dim ceiling without really seeing it. Unfair. She couldn't shake the thought. It was all so unfair.

But did it have to be? Could she still salvage something from this mess? If she didn't do something, no one else would on her behalf.

Veshwa was the key to finding her family. Veshwa might even be her own mother. If she was a servant of Veyle, it seemed logical that Saroya would find her in the capital. She *had* to go with the others to U'Veyle.

Saroya threw back her blanket, and swung her legs over the edge of the bed, moving quietly so as not to wake Nalini. She padded barefoot across the floor, then thought better of it. Best to put her best foot forward. She returned to the bed, and fumbled beneath it, looking for her sandals. She grabbed the shoes, and worked her way back to the door.

"Where are you going?" Nalini asked, voice muzzy with

sleep.

"Best you don't know."

"That doesn't bode well." Nalini sounded wide awake now.

Saroya slipped on her sandals, since stealth no longer gained her anything. "The doyenne's mad at me already, right? I might as well do something to really embarrass her in front of her guests."

"Saroya!" But Saroya had already started down the hall. She heard the rustling of sheets, then the slap of feet coming after her. Nalini tugged at her hand, but kept her voice low to avoid waking the others. "Tell me what you're doing."

"I'm going to talk to that man."

"The king's guardsman?" Nalini's voice pitched up two octaves. "What for?"

"You don't have to come with me." Saroya paused. "On second thought, it might be helpful if you did, but I won't force you to."

Nalini bit her lip in the dim corridor. "If the doyenne catches us …"

"I'll say I dragged you after me." Saroya arrived at the stairs. "So. Are you coming?"

Nalini hesitated but followed Saroya down the stairs. They exited the dormitory building and crossed the courtyard to a smaller building that housed infrequently used guest quarters. Despite the late hour, lantern light still flickered in several windows. Saroya hoped her quarry was in one of those rooms. She eased open the outer door, and entered the building. A long corridor with a series of identical doors lay before her. Suddenly her plan seemed half-baked, even to her. How would she find him without waking everyone up?

"Can I help you?" The deep voice sounded right in Saroya's ear. She stifled a startled squeak, and turned to find one of the guardsmen studying her. He did not look amused to find two girls traipsing about.

Saroya shored up her courage. "We're looking for your leader."

"Captain Callor? At this hour? What could you possibly —"

Saroya interrupted him before her nerve failed and she turned tail and ran. "My friend here has a question about the journey to the city." Nalini's eyes bugged out.

"It can't wait until morning?"

"No. She needs to send word to her parents before she leaves and won't have time to write in the morning."

It felt like such a slim excuse, but Saroya gave him her best pleading look. Beside her, Nalini fidgeted.

The guard sighed. "Fine. Follow me." He led them to the door at the end of the hall, and knocked. "Captain? You have visitors."

The door opened. The tall man who stood in the doorframe took them in with single assessing glance that lingered on Saroya before he turned to her roommate. "Nalini Ferlen, if I remember correctly?" His voice was soft but authoritative.

"Yes, that's me."

"I am Eiden Callor. What can I help you with?" The other guardsman moved back to his post by the entrance. Callor continued. "It's late and we start a long ride tomorrow."

Nalini nodded, with little enthusiasm. Saroya knew Nalini was not the most accomplished rider. "Umm ... Well, my friend ..." Nalini looked like she wanted to sink into the stone floor.

Saroya risked a timid "Sir?"

Callor turned. "And who are you?"

Saroya swallowed. What must he think of her flight from the dining hall? She looked down at her feet. "Saroya Bardan," she muttered.

"Speak up, girl."

She looked up, met his eyes—grey, like flint.

"You have something to say? I have little time to waste."

"I would like to go with you to U'Veyle."

Nalini gaped at her.

"You are the same age as your friend?"

"Yes."

"And you will be leaving the Adepts this coming spring?" Saroya nodded. "Then why are you not already on Doyenne Ganarra's list of students making the journey?"

Saroya flushed and looked down again. Why must he make her say it? She took a deep breath and looked him in the eye.

"I'm Untalented." She felt queasy, as she saw all the days ahead of her when she would have to repeat those words to men such as him. All the doors closing.

"I see."

Do you really? He watched her still, and though she most wanted to disappear, she held his gaze. "The doyenne does not believe I will benefit from any higher learning in the capital," she admitted. "I'll work for my keep if I have to— cook, take care of the horses, anything. Please ... I need to go with you."

His eyes narrowed, and she thought he would speak again. Instead, he shook his head slightly. "In the courtyard at dawn," he said to Nalini. Then he shut the door in their faces.

Saroya stared at the wood in front of her. She couldn't look at Nalini. She turned and headed back to the dormitory, felt moisture on her cheeks. Nalini put her arm around Saroya's shoulders.

Saroya's voice quavered. "I guess that's that, then."

CHAPTER 3

The grey light of dawn brightened the sky as Saroya waited in the hallway outside Doyenne Ganarra's chambers. Bridles jingled in the courtyard below the window, and stable hands shouted as they saddled recalcitrant mounts. Nalini had run off to grab a quick breakfast before the travellers left. *Without me*, Saroya thought.

The doyenne's assistant poked her head out into the hallway. "You may enter now."

Saroya slipped past the heavy wooden doors. All of last night's jokes about punishments aside, Saroya was quite sure the doyenne could make the rest of her stay uncomfortable, if not unbearable, if she felt a transgression was large enough. Worse, what if she kicked Saroya out right now?

The assistant held open the door to the doyenne's inner chamber. Saroya kept her expression neutral as she curtsied before the large desk in the centre of the room. The watery dawn light silhouetted Doyenne Ganarra against the windows, the candle sconces not bright enough to illuminate her countenance.

The doyenne steepled her fingers underneath her chin. The silence lengthened. Saroya shifted her feet. Finally, the doyenne sighed.

"I summoned you here, child, to chide you. It was unforgivably rude to leave the dining hall in front of our guests. Disappointments are many in life and you need to learn how to handle them." Doyenne Ganarra paused, pursing her lips. Saroya steeled herself for the expected lecture. "Instead I find myself having to reward you."

Saroya blinked.

"The edict is clear," came a voice from behind her. Startled, Saroya turned—Eiden Callor stood in the far corner in front of a bookshelf. "All students completing their studies in the spring are to journey to U'Veyle."

"To pursue their Talents with their guilds. This one has no Talent. I interpreted—"

"I don't have the luxury of interpretation. Talented, Untalented, rich, poor, fair, ugly—none of these words appear on the parchment I gave you. 'All students.' Those are the only words I care about."

No one spoke. The words whirled around inside Saroya's head, gibberish consonants and vowels, until their meaning coalesced. She gaped at the doyenne. "You mean—?"

"Yes, child. You are going to the capital. Eiden Callor is pressed to leave. Go and get your things together." The doyenne shook her head.

Saroya hurried from the room. She dipped a curtsy to Callor, who nodded as she passed. U'Veyle! She was going to U'Veyle. Entering the hall, she found herself grinning for what felt like the first time in days, despite Doyenne Ganarra's parting words.

"Such a waste."

∞ ∞

Saroya and her mount had come to an uneasy truce. After riding with the convoy for a week, the long hours in the saddle bothered her less. The stables contained slim pickings for mounts when she rushed in the morning they started out. Her only options: an old, tired mare who would as soon bite you as let you saddle her, or a young gelding notorious for shying without warning.

She still wondered if the mare wasn't the better bargain. The gelding spent the first day balking at every noise in the bush, or every shout of the king's men. "Control your horse, or move him to the back of the group," Eiden Callor ordered. She hung back from then on.

Nalini kept her company. She chattered away while bumping along in her saddle, gripping the pommel in one hand while her other sawed the reins from side to side. Saroya felt sorry for Nalini's horse.

At twilight, they would make camp in a meadow, or a hostelry if they happened to arrive at a village by sunset. Eiden Callor, with his men seasoned travellers, would not stop at any town for convenience. It didn't matter if they passed a comfortable-looking inn in late afternoon. He would press on until darkness. Then he chivvied them up again at dawn to continue the journey.

Tonight, they stopped in a small clearing at the side of the road, after travelling all day through wooded countryside. Some students muttered complaints, but one disdainful glance from Callor silenced even the worst grumbler. All except for Martezha. Saroya had never heard such bleating in her life. "The ground's too hard." "This food is disgusting!" "The cold night air is damaging my singing voice. How can I possibly impress my guild if I arrive hoarse? Not to mention exhausted, I mean, can nothing be done about the infernal snoring?"

"Maybe your precious vocal cords would work better if you opened your mouth less." Had she said that out loud? Saroya shot a glance at Martezha, who just continued grousing.

Saroya unsaddled and hobbled the horses while Nalini went to get water and light the fire. This had been their routine ever since the first night, when Martezha told Saroya to get away from her campfire. "Go make your own, useless. You should be preparing us dinner." And that set the tone for the trip. The others followed Martezha's lead and shunned her as well. Without Nalini's help, Saroya would be eating cold rations.

By the time Nalini and Saroya started preparing their meagre fare, the king's men had already eaten and begun patrolling the camp's perimeter. Any excuse to avoid

Martezha and her friends. The men were careful not to get dragged into fetching and carrying for her. Besides, brigands took advantage of the unwary.

Saroya unrolled their bedding while Nalini roasted the hare. She stood up, kneading the small of her back.

Nalini looked up from the pot. "What are you going to do when we arrive in U'Veyle?"

"Find a room somewhere and then get my bearings? There's got to be plenty of work out there."

Nalini divided up the meat, and they tucked into the food.

"I've been meaning to ask you, Nalini ... Building was one of my better subjects—"

"That doesn't mean anything now."

"At any rate, I was wondering ... Would your family maybe sponsor me for the Builder's Guild?"

Saroya held her breath. A favour was one thing, but this ... Nalini seemed to have come upon a tough piece of meat. When she finally swallowed her mouthful and spoke, her voice was flat.

"You want me to tell them you're a guild-worthy builder."

"Your family is so well known among the builders. If they vouch for me, the guild is sure to accept me."

"I can't do that, Saroya."

"Why not? I know how to build."

"Building isn't just putting planks and stones together, or drawing interestingly shaped houses. The guild will see through you in a second. You're asking me to lie for you."

"I'm not! If I can just get my foot in the door, I'm sure someone will apprentice me."

"It's bad enough I'm not following the family tradition of building. If my parents found out I lied to them over something like this—they'd disown me."

"But—"

"No. Don't ask me again."

Saroya stalked off to the stream to rinse the dishes. She understood Nalini's misgivings, but it was just ... Gah! She wanted to scream. Even her best friend wouldn't lift a finger to help. How was she supposed to make her way in the world, when everybody refused to look beyond the fact of her Untalent? Was a small fudging of the facts so awful when set against an entire life wasted?

When she got back, Nalini was wrapped in her bedroll, asleep, or maybe just pretending. Saroya turned in as well, but sleep didn't come easily.

∞ ∾

Saroya awoke, disoriented. The moon had set and the campfire embers glowed a dull red. Men shouted and horses whinnied in fear. She threw off her blanket. The clashing clang of weapons shot fear down her spine, and her stomach clenched. Nalini crouched by the fire.

"Bandits, I think," Nalini whispered. "What do we do?"

In the dark, soldier, thief, and student were indistinguishable. Except for the king's men, none of the travellers had weapons.

Saroya made a quick decision. "Let's get the horses to the woods."

Nalini's wide eyes glistened at her from across the fire. "What?"

"We're better off out of the action. Keep your mare between you and the fighting. Grab a piece of wood from the fire and if anybody tries to hurt you, skewer them with it."

"Are you crazy?"

"Got a better plan?"

Saroya grabbed her horse's halter and sliced through his hobble with her belt knife. Keeping a calming hand on the bridge of his nose, she led him off to nearby scrub. Stumbling in the gloom, Nalini followed close behind. A few yards into the woods, the sounds of fighting faded. Saroya stopped and handed the gelding's lead to Nalini.

Cocking her head, Saroya listened to the night sounds for a few moments. Good. Nobody had followed. "Stay here and keep the horses quiet."

"Where are you going?"

"Back to bring others."

"Saroya, it's too dangerous!"

"I'll be careful."

She slipped off in the direction of the struggle.

Peering out into the clearing from behind a tree, Saroya could make no sense out of the scene. Horses milled about, straining at their hobbles. Several boys screamed, and a few girls cried hysterically. At least two groups of men fought, but Saroya could not tell soldier from enemy.

Saroya fought to control her breathing, and the urge to hightail it back to Nalini. There! On her left, the dying glow of a campfire backlit Tarmi's blocky silhouette. Tarmi the Fat excelled at battle and military strategy, although given his well-deserved nickname, Saroya could not imagine him as a soldier. Then again, the Adepts of the Cloister were not versed in the arts of war—Tarmi had been over the moon at the prospect of training in U'Veyle, with the king's hosts.

Tarmi had encircled a small knot of girls with their horses, and waved a large stick back and forth in front of him, warning off potential attackers. Saroya crept around the edge of the clearing, drawing even with his group. She snuck out of the woods and crouched behind a large, fallen trunk. She tossed a rock at Tarmi's feet. He whirled to face her, brandishing his stick in front of him.

"Tarmi, it's Saroya," she hissed at him.

"Quick, get in the circle."

"Nalini's hidden in the woods. I can take these girls there. They'll be safe. But we have to be quiet."

Tarmi glanced at the main fight, then back at her. He nodded then ducked into the circle of horses. She heard whispering then a frightened girl appeared, leading a small roan mare.

Tarmi jogged up to her. "Where in the woods?" Saroya gave him rough directions. "Good. I'll see if I can gather any others. Meet me back here."

Saroya shushed the three girls then gestured for them to

follow her. After a brief trek, Nalini's pale face loomed out of the darkness. Saroya sensed more than saw her relief. Leaving the girls with Nalini, she headed back to Tarmi. He waited for her at the edge of the clearing, with four more students, but he hadn't escaped unscathed. Blood from a cut on his cheek dripped onto his tunic.

"It's nothing," he replied to her question. "I misjudged someone in the dark. Thought it was Callor. Managed to cut me before I whacked him over the head with the log. Guess he misjudged me." Tarmi grinned at her. "But now I've got this." He held up a short sword then glanced back at the waiting group. "I told them to leave the horses this time. Too close to the action for disappearing mounts to go unnoticed." He turned and pushed one of the waiting girls towards Saroya. She grabbed the girl's wrist to lead her off.

"Don't touch me you filthy Untalent!" Martezha's shriek resounded across the clearing. Saroya flinched. Tarmi's head whipped around.

"Will you shut up? You'll get us all killed!" Saroya hissed.

Martezha ripped her arm out of Saroya's grasp. "Tarmi … are you going to let this scum speak to me like that?"

Tarmi shrugged. "Go with her or not, but don't come whining to me when you get your head lopped off. I'd take her advice and shut your yap if I were you." He jogged off into the darkness to find more students. Saroya hurried into the woods with the three others before any brigands could pinpoint Martezha's voice. She almost wished Martezha wouldn't come to her senses, but the singer hurried after them. Nothing like being alone in the dark to change one's mind.

With two more trips, they rounded up a dozen students. The next time Saroya returned to the clearing, no one waited for her. She squinted at the skirmish. Two clusters of men still fought, grunting with each parried blow, but now Saroya could make out Tarmi's large form. He was surprisingly light on his feet. The huddled shadows on the ground must be either injured or frightened students. She clenched her fists, and wished for a weapon. She wouldn't know what to do with it, but at least she wouldn't feel so vulnerable.

Abruptly, it was all over. One man let out a last hoarse cry, then several shapes milled about, prodding the slumped figures at their feet. Should she stand up? A large shadow separated itself from the tree to her right. Startled, she spun around.

"C'mon. All's clear. Let's go get the others." Tarmi followed her into the woods as she tried to slow her breathing.

Arriving back at the camp, rescued students in tow, they found Eiden Callor's men relighting the campfires and tending to their wounded. Nalini searched for her stash of healing herbs in her saddlebag. Two of the five soldiers were hurt, neither seriously, but the brigands' horses had trampled two students, and blows felled two more. Nalini enlisted help setting a broken arm, so she could tend to a bleeding head wound.

Saroya was applying a poultice to Tarmi's cut when Eiden

Callor found them.

"You did well, Tarmi. A bit rough with your sword handling but the right instruction will improve that. I will see to it that Master Kivik speaks with you when we arrive in U'Veyle." Tarmi beamed with pride at the mention of the king's swordmaster. "Good thinking removing the others from the battle. They were safer in the woods."

Tarmi glanced at Saroya. "Actually, sir, I can't take credit for that. It was her idea."

"Indeed?" Callor looked at her with frank surprise. "Well done."

Saroya shot Tarmi a grateful look. Someone thought she'd done something right!

Sleepless tossing and turning plagued the camp for the rest of the night. Every branch swishing in the breeze sounded like reinforcements sneaking up to avenge their dead comrades.

The next morning the soldiers laid out the bodies of ten brigands in a row at the edge of the clearing. Callor's men built rough cairns. They saddled up, Callor giving the bodies one last contemptuous glance. "We'll have to let the local council in the next town know about these."

They entered the low foothills of the coastal mountains. Callor planned three days to wind their way through the passes, but their wounded hampered their progress. Saroya didn't mind. She preferred her mount's slower walking gait to his jouncy trot, and the slow pace kept Nalini relaxed. They avoided the topic of last evening's conversation.

The rugged wildness of the passes took Saroya's breath away. She had never seen mountains such as these. Unlike the gentle rolling embrace of Adram Vale's hills, the coastal range thrust upward, daring travellers to pass. Snow capped the peaks and eagles screeched, circling high above, spying out fish in the alpine streams. They climbed higher, and a chill settled into the air. Saroya dug her cloak out of her saddlebags. At night, she and Nalini huddled together for warmth. The king's men remained unfazed by the cold.

At midday on their third day through the mountains, after they spent the morning leading their horses up a narrow goat path, Callor stopped and turned around to face them. "We have reached the peak. It grows warmer from here." They picked their way down until the track widened. Downhill was more difficult in some ways than up. By the end of the day, Saroya's knees ached, and her muscles stiffened from trying to keep her balance on the loose shale. Callor was right, though: by the next morning, she no longer needed her cloak. A tangy breeze replaced the crisp alpine air. Saroya couldn't identify the smell yet.

They rounded the flank of a hill a day later and the coast opened up before them. That strange smell must be the ocean's salt aroma. It was so big! Far off in the distance, the white sails of a trading ship shimmered on the edge of the blue expanse. Closer in, the eastern foothills tapered off onto a low-lying plain. Where land met ocean, the pink-yellow stones of U'Veyle's towers rose up. From the northwest, the great river Aghrab poured down from its humble beginnings in the interior of Veyle. U'Veyle sprawled across the Aghrab Delta, stone bridges and canals criss-crossing its many tributaries and backwaters. Saroya drank in the sight.

"Impressive, no?"

Saroya started at the voice beside her. Eiden Callor sat astride his mount, gazing down at the city.

"It's beautiful."

"Before the Founders came, nothing existed here but marsh and bog. All the buildings are on piles, driven deep into the mud."

"Why go to so much trouble?"

"The marshes are impassable without a local guide. Makes it hard for an army to invade."

"I've never been anywhere so ... so grand. I've never been outside Adram Vale."

Callor allowed a small smile to lift the corners of his mouth. The softening of his features made him appear younger than she'd judged until now. "I think you'll enjoy U'Veyle. A clever person can find plenty of opportunity."

"Clever, maybe. But Untalented?"

"Quick wits and an industrious nature can overcome many obstacles."

He nudged his mount with his heels and moved towards the front of the convoy, leaving Saroya pondering his words, and why he would bother giving advice to one such as her.

They trailed down from the pass and joined the main north-south coast road. Farmers and merchants carting their wares into the capital drew aside to make way for the king's men. Their motley and bandaged charges drew curious stares. Saroya stared right back, fascinated. Shepherds in homespun woolens herded their flocks up roads shared by noblemen's carriages driven by liveried coachmen. A rich merchant in a fur-trimmed cloak rode a fat mare in the opposite direction. He followed a cart piled high with wine casks.

The grassy plain soon graduated to marshy bog. Rushes lined the raised road. Saroya marvelled that such a road, so straight and dry, was even possible in soggy terrain like this. In a pool off to the side, a heron, immobile on its stilt-legs, fixated on its fishy prey. Saroya hoped the fish escaped the trap, like she'd escaped the mines.

They arrived at the South Bridge, a massive structure crossing over the southernmost arm of the Aghrab River. The clatter of the horses' hooves on stone changed into a muffled clop over the wooden centre span. It could be raised to deny entry to the city. Eiden Callor hailed the watchman, who waved them through. The babble of conversation echoed off the walls as they passed beneath the imposing arched gate. The students clustered their mounts closer together, like a herd of deer closing ranks, seeking the safety of numbers. Craned necks, wide eyes, and gaping mouths gave away the group's newcomer status.

Just beyond the arch, the main road split into three diverging forks. Callor pointed to the westernmost fork. "That's the best route to Galon Ford. It bypasses most of the city. Over that way," he pointed to the east fork, "is the port and the Vergal Quarter. You may all want to avoid that area for now. It's not known for its savoury reputation." They took the central path through the Market District.

They passed over myriad canals. How could all these people—many in hovels wedged between warehouses, barns, and storerooms—live in once place? The spicy smell of cooking foods mingled with the less pleasant odour of offal. Muddy rivulets of sewage ran down the street. Saroya wrinkled her nose at the stench.

Saroya could only gawk at the market itself. Merchant upon dealer upon peddler hawked wares everywhere she looked. The whole square teemed with people, like some great school of numberless fish. The crowds moved and flowed like fish as well, in no apparent pattern, yet somehow with no collisions either. Ahead of Saroya, Tarmi shrank back from a man clutching at his leg, proffering pastries in his other hand. Tarmi shot a pleading look at Saroya. "He won't take no for an answer!" Tarmi kicked at the flank of his horse, dislodging the seller, and moved ahead, wedging his horse between two girls' mounts. He gave one final worried glance at the man, like a mouse peeking out of its lair to ensure the cat hadn't followed.

Saroya tried to point out a jeweller's stall to Nalini, but her friend was practically bouncing in her saddle, staring off to the northeast. "Captain Callor said the Healer's Guild's down that way!"

"Soon, Nalini. Don't worry."

"It can't be soon enough!"

At another major arm of the Aghrab, the character of the city changed. The buildings grew more opulent. Harried students and apprentices on their way to full mastery of their Talents flowed through the doors of guildhalls. Family House sigils over the doors of stately mansions heralded the centuries of noble history within. "Look!" Nalini said as they rode past one particularly opulent building. "It's the headquarters of the Order of Adepts!" Saroya made a note to herself to avoid that one. She wanted as little as possible to do with Adepts these days.

The road paralleled a waterway Callor named as the Dalcen Canal. Elegant barques floated past, poled along by barquiers with House crests sewn to their livery. An ornate barque glided along in the opposite direction, and Saroya caught Martezha eyeing with envy its rich passenger's flowing silk gown. Turning to stare after the woman, Martezha would have ridden her horse right into the canal if one of Callor's men hadn't noticed and grabbed at her reins just in time.

In the middle of a five-sided plaza, cascading streams of water from a great fountain pearled in the sun's last rays. Across the canal, long shadows draped themselves over manicured topiaries and marble fountains. The bigger the houses got, the smaller Saroya felt.

The canal poured into a basin at the foot of the castle. Saroya tilted her head and admired the walls glowing in the setting sun. Pennants fluttered in the sea breeze. She straightened in her saddle—wait, were they heading there? They couldn't be heading there! Nalini stared back at Saroya, eyes as big as ten-weight coins.

"The road has nowhere else to go!" Saroya said.

Nalini agreed. "I expected a comfortable inn, before going to the guild, but U'Veyle Castle?"

Saroya looked down at her filthy travel clothes and shook her head. She looked exactly like someone's poor country cousin. So much for making a good first impression.

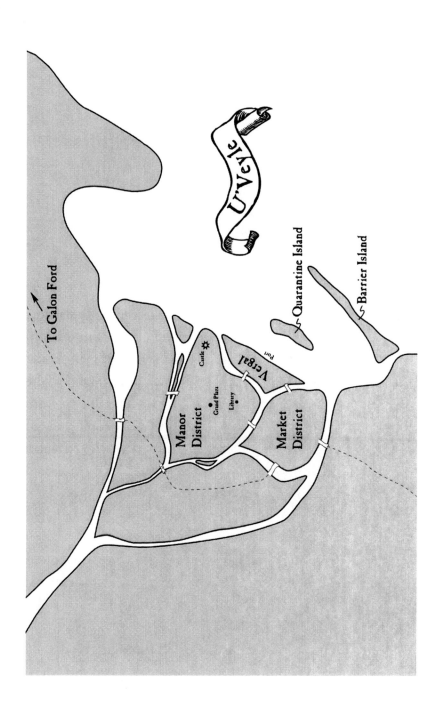

CHAPTER 4

The road arched over the basin and adjoining esplanade, where glossy varnished barques bobbed at moorings. From the esplanade, stairs rose up to the paving stones at the castle gate. Eiden Callor led the students through to the inner courtyard. Pennants bearing the royal crest hung from the walls. Stable boys came tearing out from some hidden nook to grab the horses' bridles. *So this is what being important feels like*, Saroya thought. *Don't get used to it.* Callor dismounted as a tall, thin man hurried across the cobbles to greet him. They spoke briefly then Callor turned to the gathered students.

"Master Guffin is the castle steward. He will show you to your quarters. Gather your bags. I leave you in his capable hands." Callor spun and strode away. Strangely, Saroya felt abandoned.

Master Guffin clapped his hands. "Dismount, please. I'll show you to your rooms." Bags slung over their shoulders, the students followed, not without some trepidation, as he led them out of the courtyard and into the castle proper. Saroya let her gaze roam to take in the high-vaulted ceilings, fluted columns, and marble floors as one hallway gave way into a staircase and then another corridor. Each new revealed opulence elicited a new round of oohs and aahs from her compatriots. Overwhelmed, Saroya lost her bearings.

Master Guffin gave Nalini and Saroya a room halfway down a long hall. As the sound of his footsteps receded down the corridor, Saroya and Nalini could do nothing but stare at each other in disbelief at the luxurious surroundings. The chatter of excited voices drifted out to them from the other rooms.

Saroya tossed her saddlebags to the floor and pressed her hand into her bed. Her fingers disappeared as they sank into the down coverlet. She walked to the arched window and opened the shutters. The castle wall plunged straight into a canal. U'Veyle lay spread out before her, lights coming on in windows everywhere as twilight descended upon the city. The warm glow from each lantern or candle hinted at endless possibilities within the city walls. Saroya smiled to herself. She turned to see Nalini lighting their candle.

"Do you think they made a mistake, somehow?" Nalini seemed strained.

"A mistake?"

"Well, I don't feel like I belong here, do you? I thought they'd take us to our guildhalls."

Saroya shrugged. "Doyenne Ganarra said the king wanted to honour his wife's memory. Maybe that means a speech or something. Do you suppose they'll feed us?" Saroya rummaged in her bag for some hard tack she'd saved.

A maid bustled into the room, carrying an urn filled with almond milk, another with cider, and a tray of steaming food. Saroya wondered if the castle servants were mind readers. Nothing about this place would surprise her.

"You must be tired from your trip," the maid said. "Master Guffin thought you might all prefer to have your dinners here in your rooms."

Saroya grinned at her. "You mean he thought we might be a little scruffy for the king's dining room."

The maid smiled tightly. "If you wish to wash up, there are bathing rooms at the end of the hall. I can see to your laundry. Just leave it by the door." She pointed to a reed basket.

Nalini spoke up. "How long will we be staying here?"

"A few days at most, I believe." The maid dipped a curtsy and exited the room.

Saroya and Nalini ate while the noodles and mussels were still hot then emptied their saddlebags of dirty travel clothes. Afterwards, they wandered off to find a large tub of hot water. Clean, scrubbed skin felt fantastic after living with the grime of their journey.

Once back in their room, they both felt too excited to sleep. In the end, they succumbed in short order to the softness of the pillows.

In the morning, Saroya discovered a small leather folder with a note slid underneath their door. The note instructed them to explore the city during the day; they had free rein to wander in the castle as long as they stayed away from the private wings. They should be dressed and ready for a special dinner at sunset.

Saroya and Nalini pocketed fruit for snacks then hurried down the hallway, wasting no time. "Let's go visit the market," Saroya said.

"Isn't that a little far?"

"Maybe, but the Healer's Guild's nearby." And just like that, Saroya got her way.

They hiked up the main road all the way back to Market Square. At first, Saroya found the press of people claustrophobic, but she soon relaxed. The anonymity came as a welcome relief after all the finger-pointing she'd endured at the Cloister. At least she was tall enough to see over the crowds; Nalini had to crane her neck or jump up on tiptoes to spot sights Saroya pointed out.

A canal ringed Market Square. Barges nosed up to quays like piglets to a sow. Dockhands hurried to feed the wares aboard to impatient merchants. The stalls displayed a staggering wealth of goods. Hordes of hawkers peddled shoes, jewelry, and cured beef. Street urchins ran from merchant stall to merchant stall, shooed away by wary stall keepers. Purple silks and scarlet brocades draped here gave way to shiny blown glass over there. One shop devoted itself entirely to spices—what luxury! Since they had little coin to spend, she and Nalini soon took the northeast exit from the square, crossing two canals before they found themselves in a small plaza. The Healer's Guild stood opposite.

Saroya nudged Nalini, who was taking in the pink stone facade and carved marble sigil with a rapt expression.

"We can go find the Builder's Guild if you prefer," Saroya teased, to mask her sudden stab of jealousy.

Nalini glared at her before grinning. "C'mon. Let's get lost. I'll be spending enough time here soon."

They meandered through the maze of streets and canals, choosing directions at random. In one alley, the smell of the tanners made them gag, while around another corner, they discovered a weaver's atelier with intricate tapestries hanging in the window. Saroya peered into one open door and saw row upon row of shelves stacked with tiles of every colour —sky blue, lemon yellow, pink, green and brown. They'd stumbled across the workshop of the famous Eliati, renowned for his fabulous mosaics. An artisan cut each tile into the small pieces of glass known as *tesserati*, which when combined formed the mosaics. They watched one of his apprentices withdraw a new tile from the glowing hot oven.

"I could do that!" Saroya said to Nalini. Maybe there would be opportunities in U'Veyle after all.

One of the apprentices overheard. "Are you an artist?"

"No."

"Then you can never hope to equal the Master. Off with you!"

It took several hours of wandering before they discerned

a pattern to the labyrinth of streets. Two concentric canals ringed Market Square to allow the transport of goods. Most other canals sprang from the river and flowed towards the centre of the island. Roads branched out like wheel spokes from the square, leading either off-island or more often to another square or plaza. Towards midafternoon, their feet aching, they rejoined the main road and returned to the castle.

Saroya and Nalini fretted about their lack of presentable clothes. They dug out their best skirts and tunics, but still felt frumpy and ill-prepared for a palace function. Saroya sighed as she stared at herself in the mirror.

"I guess this will have to do."

Saroya reached out, her fingers melding with her reflection's. The glass was cold. "I've never seen a mirror like this before—it looks like it's made of glass. Do you think all the rooms have them?"

Nalini shrugged. "It's certainly easier to braid hair than with my hand mirror." She held up a polished silver oval, then tossed it on the bed and reached for her hairpins. Saroya helped her work her hair into a presentable coif. She found Nalini's sleek black locks so much more elegant than her own, which threatened to degenerate into curly tangles if she left them alone too long.

"Nalini, why are you so nice to me still?"

"What kind of question is that?"

"You're the only person who doesn't treat me like a pariah. It didn't make your life any easier on the trip." Saroya tucked another pin into Nalini's hair.

"The day you came back from your Testing, you were still the same Saroya."

"But everybody hates Untalents."

"Who, Martezha? The only thing she thinks about is the pecking order. The rest of them are just sheep, they'll like or dislike anything Martezha tells them to."

"So you don't hate Untalents."

"I don't hate you. All that stuff about Untalents being thieves and liars—my mother says it's rot. Just people being mean because they know Untalents can't defend themselves. My parents taught me to respect the servants—it's not like they can help their lot—and be grateful we had people to do that type of work. Your life is going to be hard enough as it is. You don't need yet another person lording it over you all the time."

"So I'm no better than a servant to you." Saroya couldn't keep the bitter sharpness from her voice.

"That's not what I meant. You can't help what happened at your Testing. That doesn't mean I can't still be your friend."

Saroya still couldn't shake the feeling that some part of Nalini looked down on her now.

They both turned at a knock at the door. A page entered and said, "Please follow me." They joined a small stream of their peers from Adram Vale as they headed for the Great Hall. Conversation was muted. Everyone else must feel just as intimidated as Saroya did.

Groups of nobles turned to stare at them as they entered the reception hall. After a cursory examination of the new arrivals, the aristocrats resumed their discussions. Saroya tried not to gawk. The ceiling floated, seemingly unsupported, high above her head, a fresco depicting the defeat of the Ileggi at U'Jiam stretching from one end to another. Tapestries hung from the walls, their bright weaves adding colour to the pallor of the stone floor. Gilded cups and intricate silverware adorned the tables.

A servant approached offering cups of wine. Saroya took one and sipped. It tasted less sweet than the fruit wines from Adram Vale. How many new flavours would she taste in the meal itself?

She looked around, unsure what to do with herself. The page left them without introductions to the assembled nobles. Could she feel *more* like an awkward student? Martezha had managed to worm her way into a knot of nobles, laughing at some anecdote about the ancient House of Batarak and a pig. What could Martezha possibly know about House Batarak?

A horn sounded and Master Guffin entered the Hall from a corridor at the far end. In a ringing voice, he announced, "All hail and welcome His Majesty, King Urdig, Protector of the Realm of Veyle and Defender of the Great Circle of Houses."

Saroya watched and did her best imitation of the bow she observed the nobles performing as King Urdig strode into the hall. A slight lift of his hand released them from their obeisance. She blinked—she stood not twenty paces from the king—the king! For a moment she couldn't breathe. What if it was all a dream? She expected him to seem different from commoners, but except for the crown encircling his head and the gilded embroidery on his clothes, he might have been a merchant or artisan. Was that a disloyal thought? He looked tired compared to his portraits and engravings. Then again, she would be tired too if she had recently buried a loved one. Urdig climbed onto a low dais and looked out over his assembled guests.

"Welcome to U'Veyle Castle. My wife Padvai held the education of those less fortunate close to her heart. To honour her memory you will be given the opportunity to enrol in U'Veyle's guilds. You—"

A commotion at the back of the room interrupted Urdig. Eiden Callor entered the hall, intercepted by a flustered Master Guffin. They hurried to the king then huddled in conference with him. Saroya could not make out what they said, but saw the king take a parchment proffered by Callor. Master Guffin waved his hands in consternation. The king questioned his guard captain. Callor shrugged.

Nalini nudged Saroya. Even on tiptoes she couldn't see past the crowd. "What's going on?"

"I can't tell."

At a final word from the king, Master Guffin bustled out of the room, gathering a few pages as he left. Eiden Callor looked as though he wanted to protest but King Urdig waved him after Guffin as he turned to address the assembly.

"I'm afraid I must postpone this ceremony." The nobles craned their necks in curiosity, as puzzled by Urdig's actions as everybody else. "If our visitors from Adram Vale would please follow me?"

Urdig led the students to a smaller room. Saroya stood in the corner with Nalini, avoiding the muttered speculations of their peers. Soon Master Guffin and Eiden Callor reappeared, leading a group of servants carrying familiar-looking bags and trunks.

"You will recognize your luggage. I had my trusted lieutenant bring it here so that none might claim theft or other unfairness," the king said.

Saroya gave Nalini a puzzled look. Her friend shrugged in confusion.

Urdig continued. "Please locate your possessions and remove all jewelry for inspection."

Saroya sighed. At least they could not accuse her of theft: she had no jewelry anymore. She went to her saddlebags and emptied their contents on one of the long tables in front of her—clothing and travel gear, and nothing much else.

When all had rummaged through their belongings, most students either had no jewelry to speak of, or just small trinkets—family rings, a broach here and there, a fine gold chain.

Urdig strode down the line of assembled students, examining the items on the table. He stopped in front of Saroya and studied her face. His gaze lingered on her features but his expression remained unreadable.

"Show me your hands."

Saroya held out her hands. Urdig did not find what he was looking for.

"Are you wearing a necklace beneath your tunic?"

Saroya shook her head. Urdig stepped away, giving her one last glance as he considered Nalini's small pile of earrings and necklaces, before moving on.

He stopped in front of Martezha, and picked out an item from the messy pile in front of her. Saroya could not hear what he murmured to Martezha. Some great emotion crossed his face as he gazed at the object in his hand. Saroya strained to see it, but he had it cupped in his palm. Then he looked up at Martezha, kissed her on both cheeks, and embraced her, stroking her blonde hair. Martezha's eyes grew huge. For once, she looked completely taken aback.

Urdig took her hand, and led her to the door. Eiden Callor intervened. Saroya thought she heard, "... can't know if this is a trick ... wait until we can confirm ..." Urdig brushed him off, ushering Martezha through the door and back to the Great Hall. Master Guffin motioned for the students to follow and they filed into the room just as the king and Martezha mounted the dais. Saroya didn't know what to think.

"My countrymen, friends. Please join me in a moment of great joy, and welcome to U'Veyle this fine young woman, Martezha. It seems she is a long-lost ... relative of Padvai's." He slipped the object he had been holding onto Martezha's finger. The room erupted in surprised outcry. Nalini gaped at the dais. Nobles shouted in a mix of disbelief and speculation. Saroya could not take her eyes off the ring finger of Martezha's right hand—through the crowd, she thought she saw a silver band, with a small blue stone flashing and sparkling. She felt faint as her vision tunnelled in to focus on that ring. She shoved through the nobles until she could see it better.

Her ring.

She had never been more certain of anything in her life.

The hubbub died down; Urdig was speaking. Nalini, who had followed as Saroya pressed forward, apologized to the people Saroya elbowed on her way through.

"This comes as a surprise to most of you. To me as well. There can be no doubt: she wears Padvai's ring," Urdig said.

The nobles roared their appreciation. Saroya swallowed bile. She steadied herself on Nalini's shoulder. Nalini winced as Saroya tightened her grip, and shot her a worried look.

Urdig went on. "We will toast to new family. Come, I have provided a feast to celebrate."

Saroya sucked in air past what felt like a vise around her chest.

"Saroya, are you all right? You look a little green." Nalini dragged her over to a chair and pressed her into it.

Saroya could barely speak. "It's my ring."

"What?"

"The ring Martezha's wearing. The queen's ring."

"I don't understand."

"My silver ring with the blue stone. The day I came back from the village. It's my ring. The one that was stolen." She was shouting now, and people turned to stare.

Nalini knelt in front of her and looked into Saroya's outraged eyes. "Are you sure? How can you tell from here?"

"You've seen it, haven't you? You don't believe me? Look at it."

"It's not that, it's just—you hardly ever showed it to me. Wasn't it gold?"

"What do I do?"

Nalini bit her bottom lip and thought for a second. "Things are too crazy right now. Everybody's in shock—it's no use causing a scene. Let's have dinner and let Martezha have her moment in the sun. Then we can go find Eiden Callor. Maybe he'll listen."

The food was indeed a feast, but the tender meats, delicate noodles and sweet desserts all tasted like sawdust to Saroya. She watched Martezha simper and smile at the now fawning nobles. Saroya caught her eye. Yes—a look of guilt flitted across Martezha's impeccable features.

The meal finally over, Saroya darted up and dragged Nalini after her. The king was talking to Eiden Callor in a corner of the hall. After pouring a splash of cider into a goblet, Saroya ducked behind a column to eavesdrop. Nalini looked as though she would rather be anywhere else.

They heard snatches of conversation.

"… why would Padvai hide a daughter?" Callor asked. Saroya nearly choked inhaling her cider. *Daughter?*

"... Announce ... heir ... Houses must know," Urdig said.

"At least wait until we send to Adram Vale to find out more."

"... Rumours ... can't wait long."

The two men moved away as a noble dragged them off to discuss the effect moving the boundaries of his estate would have on his taxes.

Nalini poked Saroya, jolting her out of her stunned silence. "Did I hear what I thought I heard?"

"They don't think Martezha's just any old relative. The ring makes her ..."

"You mean, makes you the queen's daughter."

"Who's going to believe that? I mean—how's it even possible?"

They went in search of Eiden Callor. Saroya spotted him in conversation with a striking dark-haired woman. He leaned against a marble column, frowning at her last words. He glanced away in irritation, and Saroya caught his eye.

"Captain Callor, may we speak with you?"

The woman looked down her nose at Saroya. "My dear, we are in the middle of an important discussion. Come back later."

Saroya flushed but dipped a quick curtsy, trying to appease. "Beg pardon, My Lady, but I must speak with Captain Callor. It's urgent."

Nalini plucked at her sleeve in warning as Callor raised an eyebrow.

"I am the queen's sister and whatever your business with him, it can wait. Go return to that rabble you arrived with."

Saroya clenched her teeth together and bit back a reply. The woman didn't sound like someone who would welcome an Untalent into the family. Nalini shifted uncomfortably and tried to drag Saroya away.

"Isolte." Callor's features betrayed no emotion. "While I see your point, it is not my place to discuss tonight's protocol with you. Better to take your complaint to Master Guffin. Please excuse me." He moved away, then, as an afterthought, turned to Saroya and Nalini. "Master Guffin informed me that your mare pulled up lame, Nalini. I am off to see the stable master now. Join me?"

They scurried after him without waiting to hear Isolte's protestations. They caught up to him at a small alcove down the hall.

"What's wrong with Doni? She was fine yesterday ..."

Callor shook his head at Nalini. "Nothing's wrong with your horse. Although you could use something for your gullibility." He turned to Saroya. "What is it? I only have a moment."

Saroya let out a grateful breath, and collected her thoughts. How to broach this?

"My lord—"

"Captain."

"Captain." She swallowed. "The ring the king found in Martezha's pile."

Nalini darted worried glances back and forth from Callor

to Saroya. Saroya's courage left her and she nearly fled. Nalini nodded in encouragement.

"What of it? Speak up, girl."

Saroya steeled herself and looked him in the eye. "The queen's ring. It is silver, with a blue stone, and knotwork etched around the band. The inscription on the inner rim reads 'Ashra, welcome to Roshan—Airic'."

Callor frowned. "Martezha has shown you this ring before?"

"I know that ring like I know my own hands. The Adept who gave it to me said it came from my mother."

Callor stepped toward her. She drew back, intimidated, Callor's no-nonsense manner now menacing. "I have no use for schoolgirl pranks." He brushed past her.

"Please, Captain! I beg you—"

He rounded on her. "Beg. Yes—that is exactly what you'll be doing when Guffin hears of this and puts you out on the street where you belong. I had thought better of you."

Saroya babbled as her hold on the situation slipped. "You don't understand—"

"I understand all too well. Did you really think this scheme would work?"

"It's not a scheme!"

"Then explain why, if the ring is yours, it was not in your possession."

"It was stolen from my room at the Cloister two months ago."

"How convenient. Did you report this theft?"

"Nalini tried to, but the Adepts wouldn't listen."

He turned to Nalini. "Can you confirm it is the ring you saw tonight?"

Nalini's anguished look took away all Saroya's hope. "No. I don't know. The stone was blue. I can't remember for sure."

Saroya held out one last possibility. "The Adepts. They can tell you!"

"The Adept who gave you the ring can verify all this?"

Saroya shook her head. "No, she died last year. But Doyenne Ganarra or someone else at the Cloister likely knows."

"You waste my time. If you had some proof ... but, no." Callor turned to go. "If I hear so much as a whisper of this tale from anybody in the castle, I will personally see to it that neither of you are welcome in U'Veyle again."

CHAPTER 5

Loric seethed beside Isolte in the carriage on the way home.

She tried to placate him with news of their son. "The Adepts sent Oran back from his latest Testing."

"And?"

"Commerce and trade. Like me." He could see the relief in her face. Their son had a Talent.

The good news failed to distract Loric from his simmering anger at the man he'd sent to Adram Vale. "I'll have him flogged! Strapped to a fence and flayed within an inch of his life. Maybe that will teach the fool to do a job right."

Isolte wisely did not defend the man.

"He told me he found the ring in the Untalent's room," Loric continued. "And what do we get instead? A beautiful, accomplished singer. The Houses will just lap it up."

He drummed a hand against his thigh.

"Where's the scandal, Isolte? For all anybody knows Padvai was eccentric and wanted a child brought up outside the court." It had been done before—King Turlac a hundred years ago was so worried about assassination he did not admit to having heirs until his deathbed.

"But that was during the Darlan Revolt, dear. The Houses are united now."

"When we thought the child was Untalented, it was the perfect setup. Now? Urdig's position is even stronger than before."

Isolte smiled. "What are the odds that a red-headed Untalent among that particular group would not be my sister's daughter?"

Loric's hand stilled. "You've seen this Untalent?"

"Didn't you notice her, my love? She's the spitting image of Padvai. Different colour eyes, and wavy hair where Padvai's was straight. An educated observer would see a resemblance."

"So why did Urdig not install her in the royal apartments?" Loric asked.

"Ah, well. I followed her and her little friend when they went to plead their case to Callor. The fools never noticed." She related the scene she'd observed in the corridor.

"Do you believe her?"

"She seemed most upset. And sincere. Factor in the family resemblance ... I suspect Callor brushed her off because he recognized the implications for Urdig. Loyal to his liege, that one."

"But she has no proof."

"And neither do we."

Loric's hand resumed its insistent tapping. "She mustn't slip through our grasp. First—we must ferret out everything there is to know about this Martezha before Urdig does. Time for another emissary to Adram Vale. And time for a new ally."

∞ ∽

In the morning, Saroya sat slumped on the bed and stared at her feet without seeing them, ignoring Nalini's soft snores. Queen's daughter. Untalented. She couldn't reconcile the two.

She moved her saddlebag over to the window so as not to wake Nalini and rummaged inside for her leather letter sheaf. She removed the small piece of parchment and frowned in frustration. Veshwa. Six little letters on which hinged her fate. "Loyal servant of Veyle." What did that mean? Had her mother written the note? Or had Veshwa? Saroya knew two things: Veshwa was a woman, and that conniving little sow Martezha knew nothing about her. Was she a servant here in U'Veyle Castle? Or someone the queen knew from elsewhere? Saroya shrugged. She had a place to start. Martezha would never see her coming.

A knock at the door startled her. Nalini rubbed a sleepy hand across her eyes and sat up. Saroya opened the door to find Master Guffin waiting.

"The guildmasters will arrive shortly." He addressed

Nalini. "Mistress Ferlen, you are to present yourself in the reception hall in one hour. Please have your bags packed."

He turned to Saroya, his face stern. Saroya gave him an uncertain look. Had Callor spoken with him after all?

"I understand you have no guild, Mistress Bardan."

That was the polite way to put it. Then it hit her—Guffin, as a servant, although an elevated one, was probably an Untalent too. She nodded.

"If you wish, we have prepared a place for you with the staff of U'Veyle Castle. You must have impressed Captain Callor. He arranged it when you arrived. You will start at the bottom, but be given any necessary training."

Saroya felt Nalini sidle up to her and nudge her with her hip.

"I am grateful for the offer, Master Guffin. It's a good one, for someone like me. But I will only take it on one condition." Nalini squeaked beside her.

Guffin raised an eyebrow. "You are not in a good negotiating position but go on."

"I'd like to stay away from Martezha."

"Why?"

"I'd rather not discuss it. In Adram Vale, we were never friends, and …" She trailed off. "I just can't be in service to her, that's all."

Master Guffin looked surprised but not put out. "Very well. I do not know if she will remain at the castle, but I won't place you among her handmaidens—you're too inexperienced. The stable staff is more appropriate. Callor told me you handled horses well. Collect your things, and I will take you to your quarters after I've seen the other students off to their guilds." He left them to their packing. So she hadn't escaped the stables after all. Maybe castle manure smelled better.

Saroya wasn't sure how, but Nalini managed to look glum and excited all at once.

"I guess this means good-bye," Nalini said.

"You won't be going far, will you? I can visit you at the guildhall on my free days—if I have any. We can write to each other if you wind up somewhere outside the city."

"I can't promise I'll be able to help, but if you ever need anything, you'll come see me, right?"

"I could have used your help last night," Saroya countered.

Hurt shadowed Nalini's eyes. "Please don't."

"How did you expect me to feel? It was the one time when I needed you to be there for me."

"If I hadn't been completely sure, it would have come out at some point and then we'd both be in bigger trouble."

"Do you always have to be such an honest prig?" Nalini looked so offended that Saroya immediately regretted her words. But Nalini hadn't just lost her family to theft. "I lied for you!"

"When?"

"That time your parents came to visit. You begged me not to tell them about your healing classes."

"That was different. And it wasn't even really a lie. It was avoiding the truth."

"So it's fine when your life is at stake, but not the other way around? Thanks for nothing." Identifying the ring as hers wasn't even a real lie. Not if it supported the truth. But she wouldn't win this argument with Nalini. Approaching Callor had taken all Saroya's courage. Could she really expect quiet little Nalini to rise to such an occasion? Still. Nalini *knew* the ring belonged to her. "Whatever. Have it your way."

"I don't want us to say good-bye like this. Stay strong."

"I'll be fine. I just have to stay out of Martezha's way. She'll want me as far from here as possible."

"It'll all work out in the end. You'll expose her for the little thief she is. I can't believe you're a princess."

Nalini reached out to squeeze her hand, but Saroya avoided the touch, still upset. "It won't do me any good unless I can prove it to someone. It may not mean anything even then."

"Why not?"

"An Untalent on the throne? Not likely."

∞ ∞

Saroya took stock of her new quarters. A narrow bed hugged the wall, with folded sheets and blankets atop a lumpy pillow. Two other beds lined the other two walls. Each bed had a nightstand at its head, and a small chest at its foot. Hooks lined the wall over the beds, her hooks empty, tunics and livery hanging from the others. A ceiling lantern provided feeble illumination—the small window in the corner let in little light. A whiff of hay and manure filtered in from the stables below.

She dropped her saddlebags on the chest and took the stack of clothing from Mistress Weeda.

"These will do you until you are fitted," the head of the castle servants said. "See the seamstress on your first free day." Mistress Weeda sized her up with an appraising eye. She pursed her thin lips then shook a bony finger at Saroya. "We punish laziness and impertinence here—how we treat you is up to you. Follow me. I'll show you where to find your meals." Mistress Weeda led her to the kitchens, where a flustered cook and several scullery maids met them. Saroya had never seen a kitchen so clean. A chorus of voices clamoured for Mistress Weeda's attention.

"It wasn't my fault—"

"I told you berry sugar—"

"Ruined, just ruined, what'll they be having for dessert now?"

Saroya gaped as Mistress Weeda sorted out the whole sorry mess then herded her out of the kitchen. "Always a crisis with that lot."

"Mistress Weeda, may I ask a question?"

"Be swift about it. The stable awaits."

"Have you ever heard of a castle servant named Veshwa?"

"I'm afraid not. If such a person ever worked here, it was before my time. Now, off to the stable with you. The head groom's expecting you." She bustled away in search of another problem to fix.

Saroya grunted in disappointment. Finding this Veshwa would not be so easy after all.

∞ ∞

"Lord Dorn, are you implying that King Urdig is intentionally concealing an Untalented child in a bid to retain power?"

Daravela, High Eminence of the Order of Adepts, stared at Loric. Though she kept her expression neutral, he could tell his words had shocked her to the core. She was known for her shrewdness, though, and he didn't doubt that she'd already analyzed the implications and potential opportunity for the Order.

"No. I don't believe he knows of the other child, Eminence," said Loric.

"Do you have proof of her identity?"

"It is only a matter of time before I do."

"Then why come to the Order with this information now?"

"I propose an alliance. The support of the Order in exchange for certain powers I will be in position to grant once I gain the throne."

"What makes you think you can unseat Urdig?" Daravela steepled her fingers.

"Once we unmask this girl, Urdig can be made to look complicit. Failing that, he looks like a fool. Taken alone, not enough to bring him down. But combined with his reaction to a few crises I intend to manufacture ..." Loric leaned forward, leaving the thought hanging. Through the window behind Daravela, he saw grey-clad Adepts sitting on the lawns below, surrounded by clusters of teaching apprentices.

"And in return?" Daravela asked.

"The Order gets a seat in the Great Circle of Houses. Full voting rights."

"And a seat for each guild."

"Impossible."

Daravela stared him down.

Loric grimaced. The Houses would fight dilution of their power. He'd need to call in all his favours. Finally he inclined his head. "Very well. Guild seats, too. I can count on your discretion?"

Daravela nodded. She pressed gnarled hands onto the armrests of her chair, and seemed to will herself upright. Loric studied her as she shambled to the window and her gaze settled onto the distant pink stones of the castle. All the eminences preceding her had failed in their attempts to consolidate the Order's power after the Great Plague. Power he'd now placed within her grasp. He hoped he wouldn't regret it.

Daravela summoned her assistant. "Contact the doyenne in Adram Vale. She is to assist Lord Dorn's inquiries and then relay all information to the Order here in U'Veyle. Any other requests regarding either Martezha Baghore or Saroya Bardan are to be deflected. Any requests. Including royal ones."

"You know this borders on treason," Loric said.

"A calculated risk. Something bothers me about this Untalent in the Roshan family line." Daravela turned back to the assistant. "And bring me all records of House Roshan Testings for the past three generations. Tell no one."

∾ ∽

Saroya scratched her nose, leaving a smear of grain dust across her cheek. She puffed a strand of hair away from her face as she poured the oats into the trough. The head groom had no use for her as a trainer, and put her to work feeding the horses and mucking out stalls, muttering "those that gets foisted on me best not expect the pretty jobs." Saroya wasn't yet trusted to ride, but so much tack needed cleaning, with all the leather to soap and metal bits to polish, that her day was full.

The feeding and stalls were her job when she first rose prior to dawn. If a large party of guards returned from a long patrol, she could spend her whole day in the barn, currying, combing, and settling the animals, never seeing the sun. She'd get back to her room in the early evening, sweaty and dusted with hay or smeared with muck. Her hair absorbed a semi-permanent odour of manure and saddle soap.

The head groom shouted at her from the door to the barn.

"Just me luck—His Majesty returns tonight and we have no carrots. He dotes on that stallion of his ... Cook says the kitchens are out as well. Go to market to fetch me a dozen."

What luck! Saroya treasured these excursions. She only got one free day a month, and used it to explore the city. If she was quick, she could complete her errand and visit the library without leaving him the wiser. She wiped her face with the cloth she used to polish the saddles and took the coin pouch the groom held out.

"Don't dawdle. You'd better account for all the coins I gave you. And behave. Your own personal ... situation is bad enough—I don't know what possessed Weeda to think taking on an Untalent was a good idea."

Saroya gritted her teeth. The groom's incessant sniping wore thin. Saroya knew she stood at the bottom of the pecking order. She'd had it with his need to rub it in.

"What does my 'personal situation' have to do with anything? Everyone here is in the same boat."

His normal expression of contemptuous disdain hardened with fury. "You dare? I am nothing like you. Come from a long line of proper weavers, I do. I'll get back into the guild when I've paid my penance."

Saroya gaped at him. "But—"

He cut her off. "Cook's a proper member of the Chef's Guild, Danno the coachman is a builder whose designs are simply not in fashion—or so he says—and Breea can no longer be a tanner since she breaks out in hives when she gets near the tanning vats—not her fault she can't do what she was born to."

Saroya squeaked out, "I'm the only Untalent here?"

"And anything you do in castle livery reflects on all of us. Now fetch those carrots."

Saroya stood stunned in the courtyard, staring at the groom. The castle servants were not Untalented, but instead, failed Talents. Failed Talents were unheard of in Adram Vale: so few people lived in the village that the need for whatever Talent a child demonstrated allowed a failure to get by. Apparently failure as a Talent did not confer greater empathy for the plight of an Untalent.

It came out of Saroya before she could stop it. "Does it make you feel better?"

The groom frowned.

"About yourself. Does bringing me down somehow make your own failures bearable?"

He glared at her and slammed the stable door.

Saroya darted out to the courtyard. It had taken her a few weeks, but she now understood the castle's labyrinthine layout. A simple rectangular structure enclosed the central courtyard. The complex network of stairs, corridors and arcades housed all the living quarters for the royal family and their servants, storerooms, and stables. Not to mention all the offices of the government, and the Hall of the Great Circle of Houses, which she had yet to see. She made her way to the west gate and set off down the road to Market Square.

As she walked she turned the encounter with the groom over and over in her head. If Untalents in the city couldn't even be servants, how did they live? She'd heard tales of the poverty and squalor in the Vergal Quarter. Perhaps it was just at the castle that Untalents weren't allowed. Which didn't bode well for her reception once she'd exposed Martezha. If she ever stood in Martezha's place, she'd make other Untalents welcome at the castle. After all, wasn't she now proving herself just as capable as the other grooms? Saroya smiled to herself as Market Square came into view.

Resisting the fascination of the constant bustle of the market, she made short work of the carrot purchase and trotted back along the main road to the Manor District. U'Veyle Library perched on a knoll within view of the castle. The imposing building dwarfed the many guildspeople who passed through its doors, researching their various fields. She hoped her castle livery would suffice instead of a guild crest. She crossed the entrance, the smell of musty paper assailing her.

Success had eluded her in accessing U'Veyle Castle's own collection of books and scrolls. Master Doga, the castle librarian, looked askance at her request, and summarily denied it. Saroya suspected he would keep even the royals out of the stacks if he could. He seemed distinctly possessive of his books.

The U'Veyle city library was another matter. Some tomes, due to age or deterioration, were accessible only to guild members who could prove a need to view their contents. Even then, a librarian supervised to ensure no further harm came to their precious charges. Most recent books were available for perusal in the reading rooms. Saroya researched the queen, to find some hint to the identity of the elusive Veshwa. This proved difficult—few histories of Queen Padvai were available, her death being so recent. She gleaned a few small pebbles of information: the queen's maiden House was Roshan, and her sister was the woman Saroya and Nalini had interrupted with Eiden Callor.

Today, Saroya wanted to find out if any of Nalini's builder relatives had drawings filed with the library. Castle stable rat was fine for keeping a roof over her head, but she could have stayed in Adram Vale for that. The only way out of the pit of Untalent was acceptance into a guild. She needed a sponsor into the Builder's Guild, and if Nalini wasn't willing to supply her with one, then she'd find one for herself.

∞ ∽

"I don't pay you to come back empty-handed."

The man standing in Loric's study shrugged. "I can only bring back what I saw. She went to the library."

"What was she looking for?"

"You 'spect I followed her in? Ain't nowhere to hide in there, and I don't even know how to pretend to read. She'd've spotted me right quick, that one."

"Maybe I should find someone who can go anywhere, then," Loric said, but grudgingly handed over a small sack of coins. This effort to track the girl on her castle excursions was getting expensive.

"Far's I can tell, she doesn't do much. Why's she so

interesting, anyway?"

"Any more questions? I can send you off to find other employment."

The man scuttled from the room. Loric pondered his options. His patience was sorely tested, but a hasty move at this point could upset his plans.

∞ ∞

Callor met King Urdig's royal barque as it pulled up to the castle esplanade. Urdig disembarked, and clasped Callor's arm in greeting. They walked up the stairs towards the gate.

"What news from Adram Vale?" asked Urdig.

"The Adepts report Mistress Baghore was abandoned as an infant at the Cloister."

Callor handed over a parchment. Dhilain of Roshan's affidavit attested to the authenticity of the ring—a betrothal gift from his father to his mother, passed down to his sister Padvai on her mother's death.

"We have no reason to disbelieve Martezha is Padvai's child, Callor."

"But is she yours?"

"Straight to the point, eh?"

"Delicacy is not why you made me guard captain."

Urdig stared at the cobblestones as they entered the courtyard. "I have no reason to doubt Padvai."

"Then why would she hide the child?"

Urdig shrugged.

"Your Majesty, if she had any reason, I must know. The

Houses won't accept Martezha as heir if they have any doubt about her lineage."

Urdig glanced around to confirm no servants lurked in their vicinity. "Enough! If I catch wind from any quarter of you pursuing further inquiries into this, I shall exile you to Kurtya, understood?"

Callor stiffened, but acquiesced.

They walked along one of the inner corridors. A tapestry of the Ileggi uprising so many years ago caught Urdig's eye. While he spent months cleaning up the mess along the southern border, Padvai had summered at the Roshan estate. She had been so happy to see him on his return. He never even knew she had conceived. It was the only timing that made sense.

They approached the arcade leading to the royal quarters. "I will issue a decree to the Houses that Martezha is my heir." Urdig ignored Callor's protestation. "The decision is final."

∽ ∾

Saroya got back to the stable to find the head groom in a tizzy. The governor of the southern city of U'Jiam had arrived unexpectedly with his entourage, and twenty mounts to unsaddle and find stalls for. Saroya worked non-stop until sunset, when she changed into clean-smelling clothes and hurried to the kitchens in search of dinner.

There, she found the governor's presence playing havoc with Cook's dinner plans. The night's simple layered flat noodle dish forgotten, the king now required a full banquet. The kitchen helpers scurried about the hot, steamy room with dishes and ingredients. An air of controlled panic wafted about with the smells of roasting meat and seafood.

Cook spotted Saroya and beckoned her over.

"Here, take this tea to the princess."

"Princess?"

"Just got word it's official. Now go on."

"But—"

"No buts. Her Highness has a sore throat and all the maids vanished into the woodwork on me. There's not a one to be found—Guffin must have them all making beds. If I don't get her this tisane soon, I'll never hear the end of it." She shoved a tray into Saroya's hands. "Off with you, now."

Saroya took a deep breath and wandered off with the tray. Until now, though it was the most direct route from the stable to the kitchens, she had avoided Martezha's wing— she was not prepared to confront her yet—so it took her a few minutes to find the right hallway. The page standing outside the door gave her a warning look.

"She's in a right foul mood today, miss. Best be done as quickly as you can." He looked askance at the door, opened it and waved her in. The new princess had not made a good initial impression on the castle servants.

Saroya stepped into the room, her curiosity warring with her resentment of Martezha. The empty antechamber opened on to an inner room through a curtained archway. A portrait of Martezha already decorated the outer room. She must have commissioned it right after their arrival in U'Veyle. What gall! In the painting, the newly minted princess, robed in scarlet velvet, sat astride an opulent white steed, staring coolly at all who entered. Saroya stuck out her tongue at the image, though she really wanted to spatter it with the tea. She shouldered aside the curtain and braved the inner chamber.

Martezha lay stretched out on the canopy bed, with her hand lying across her forehead, eyes half-closed. A handmaiden waved a fan towards the ersatz princess's face. Saroya searched out a surface on which she could leave the tray. Spotting a sideboard across from the bed, she dipped a slight curtsy at the door, and headed over to deposit the tea. Hoping she had avoided notice, she tiptoed back to the door. She gave her exiting curtsy, but Martezha's whining croak halted her.

"At least make yourself useful and pour the tea. Or is even that beyond your talents?"

Saroya's lips tightened, but she kept her annoyance in check, and her head down. She picked up the small porcelain cup from the tray. Her hands shook with repressed anger as the tea flowed out from the pot. A drop splashed onto the tray. Saroya focused on it wobbling and shimmering in the light, then gathered herself and turned to Martezha, who snatched the proffered cup from her hands. More tea spilled onto the bed.

"You clumsy fool, look what you've done!"

The handmaiden backed away and made herself as

unnoticeable as possible in the corner near the window. Saroya met Martezha's eyes—a deep satisfaction lurked in their depths. Saroya refused to give her the excuse she was looking for.

"My deepest apologies, Highness. I'll send for new bedding. If you will excuse me, I have other duties to attend to." She gave the smallest bow that courtesy required, and beat a retreat to the door. Martezha took a sip of the tea. The superior smirk turned to sudden fury. She hurled the cup at Saroya.

"It's not even warm! Do you know what cold tea will do to my voice? You stupid cow—if you made this cough worse I'll have you flogged. I'm supposed to sing for the governor tonight."

Tea dripping from her face, Saroya fumbled in her pocket for a cloth and mopped the tea from the floor, picking out the broken shards of the cup. Her breath rushed through her nostrils. She struggled to curb her bitter response. Martezha's hand slammed down on the sideboard.

Martezha turned to the handmaiden. "Tell Master Guffin that I won't tolerate this—this Untalented trash in my presence." The girl scuttled away, head bent. Martezha sneered at Saroya. "If I ever see you here again I'll make your life miserable."

Saroya ripped her gaze from Martezha's manicured fingers and the ring adorning that hand. She returned Martezha's jade stare. Something inside her snapped.

"You and I both know whose life will be miserable when

the truth comes out."

Martezha drew back as if bitten. "Get out of my sight."

"With pleasure."

Saroya gathered the tray and what was left of her dignity and left the room, refusing to hurry. The page took in her damp skirt and grinned.

"Warned you, didn't I? Better take my advice, next time."

Saroya didn't bother telling him there wouldn't be a next time. Martezha would follow through on her threat. Saroya's presence was a constant reminder of Martezha's lie. It made Saroya's plan to get into the Builder's Guild all the more urgent; Martezha would soon drum up some excuse to dismiss her from the castle staff. Her position here was too precarious.

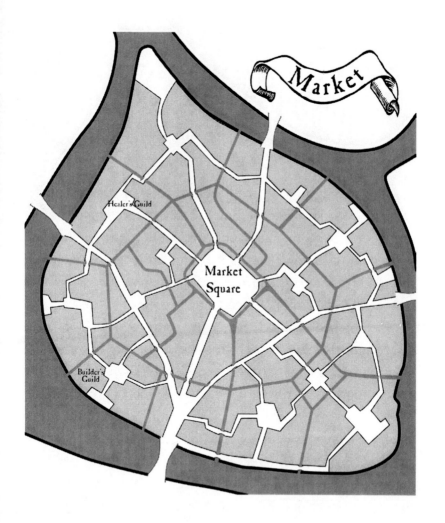

CHAPTER 6

Saroya caught her breath at the foot of the guildhall's staircase. Was she late? Getting the free day to attend Nalini's induction ceremony had been simple, but good luck finding proper attire. It took her all morning to locate someone in the castle willing to lend her a decent dress. A part of her wished she wouldn't find one—an excuse not to go.

She tucked behind her ears stray strands of hair, disarrayed from her hurried trot across the city. She couldn't afford a barque ride. To her own dismay, she couldn't resist comparing her borrowed linen dress to the fine silks of the other guests. A matron in rich furs sniffed and pulled her small daughter away from Saroya. Clean linen or not, the smell of manure defied all purging attempts from her hair. Saroya lifted her head and marched after the matron's family through the arching doorway. She had done her best and Nalini wasn't one to care much about silks.

Saroya let her curiosity at her first foray into a guildhall lead her about the atrium before she entered the auditorium for the ceremony. The marble floor cooled her feet through the thin soles of her sandals. Scattered about the area, large urns cradled exhibits of healing herbs, their therapeutic properties listed on small placards. Sculptures of famous healers throughout history lined the wall to the left of the entrance, some shown applying a poultice to or bleeding an ailing patient, others holding minerals or herbs. Saroya frowned. She could do all that. What made them so special? On the right wall, a mural depicted the sacrifices made by the healers during the Great Plague three hundred years ago.

At the far end, three arches led to various wings of the guildhall, the guild crest prominent atop the middle arch. Nalini had told her that the left hallway led to the healers' quarters, and the right to the research and teaching rooms. Saroya followed the stream of proud parents and robed healers to the middle arch. There an administrator asked to see her invitation then directed her to the guildhall's auditorium. Saroya took a seat on a stone bench.

For all the grandeur of the large hall, the Healer's Guild kept the ceremony itself simple, even though it reminded her of everything she was not. The guild candidates mounted the stage and took places behind a podium. Saroya spotted Nalini in the second row—her tiny frame just visible. The master healer made a short speech and, one by one, called each of the new apprentices to him. He led them through the Healer's Oath then placed upon each right middle finger a ring sealing their lives to the guild. Saroya had never seen anyone so happy as Nalini when the ring encircled her finger. Saroya ached for the day when a guild might accept her too. Nalini returned to take her place with the inductees, and Saroya spotted her scanning the crowd. Saroya waved and Nalini smiled back in recognition. A shadow crossed Nalini's face. Saroya wasn't certain why.

Back in the atrium, its tables now heaped high with food and drink, Saroya grabbed a goblet of cider from a server and hunted through the crowd for Nalini.

She found her in animated conversation with another new healer. Nalini kept craning her neck as though looking for someone. She noticed Saroya approaching and grinned.

"Look at you! Castle life is treating you well!"

Saroya blushed and decided not to mention her borrowed clothes. This was Nalini's night, after all.

"What about you? You're a fully fledged healer now."

"Not quite yet."

"But tonight—"

"Tonight we all became members of the guild. But I'm not allowed to set up practice on my own until a master gives his approval. Maybe as much as a full year from now."

Nalini tried to peer around Saroya without appearing to do so.

"Look, if you'd rather I not be here, just say so."

"No, no, it's great to see you, Saroya."

"Are you waiting for someone? You seem distracted."

Nalini shrugged, and ignored the question. "Are things all right for you at the castle? Martezha's not giving you a hard time, is she?"

"Martezha. Fah!" A change in subject seemed in order. "Are you allowed to show me around the guildhall?"

Nalini gave a little hop and grabbed Saroya's wrist. "Allowed? I'd love to. Come on." She extracted them from the group clustered around them and headed down the left-hand hallway. After a maze of marbled corridors inset with oaken doors, she arrived at a door three down from the end of a corridor and flung it open.

"This is my room."

Saroya peered inside. Nalini spun around with her arms outstretched. Fragrant herbs hung from a planter by a large window, books and parchment lay strewn on the desk, and shelves of medical tomes covered the walls.

"No roommate?" Saroya didn't want to think about how long she'd wait before she got a room all her own.

"No, the guild believes all members need a quiet place to study. You should see the library."

"Nalini."

"What?"

"You're hiding it pretty well but I can tell something's bothering you."

Nalini turned to the window. Had she pried too hard? Nalini's shoulders shook. Saroya hurried over. Nalini looked up at her, lips quivering, liquid pooling in the corners of her eyes.

"They didn't come."

"Who didn't come?"

"My parents. What did I expect—the whole builder thing …"

"It's a long way to U'Veyle from Galon Ford."

"They didn't even send a note. Nothing. None of the U'Veyle Ferlens showed up either."

Saroya hugged her friend.

"Nalini. You're the best healer the Cloister ever taught. It would be pointless for you to even try to be a builder. If your parents can't see how wonderful you are at healing, then they don't deserve you."

"It just hurts." Nalini's voice dropped to a whisper. "Why can't they be proud of me?"

∾ ∽

Saroya looked over her handiwork with a critical eye. She compared the letter sitting on the table in front of her, ink still drying, with the one on the bench. The calligraphy matched well, the signatures indistinguishable, with only a small squiggle out of place in one of the curlicues. Most casual observers wouldn't give it a second glance.

She blotted the parchment, then packed up her writing implements, giving the paper a few more moments to dry. The quiet corner she'd found in the library remained empty. Anybody coming in would see a girl taking notes about the book in front of her. And she had—it just wasn't her only project for the day. She felt a twinge of guilt at faking a signature, but if all went as planned, no one would ever know.

She put the parchment into her leather letter holder and turned back to the book on the stand, *A History of the Veyle Plague Years*. She riffled through her notes. Her quest to find the mysterious Veshwa led her in strange but interesting directions. None of the castle servants she discreetly probed admitted knowing anyone named Veshwa. It was not a common name; if Veshwa had been a servant of her mother's, it had not been during her tenure as queen.

She sent a letter to the doyenne in Adram Vale asking about Veshwa and whether anyone knew the story of her ring. Who had left her there as an infant? Her mother? This Veshwa? Had she been dropped off anonymously or had the Adepts spoken to whoever carried her there?

While waiting for a reply, she set out to learn more about House Roshan, her mother's maiden House. Tales of bravery in battle or service to the realm littered the history of Veyle; Houses like Dorn had made a name for themselves by defeating the attempted invasion of U'Veyle by the Ileggi when plague losses still weakened the city three hundred years ago. Unlike most current noble Houses, House Roshan's lineage stretched back even before the plague. Many of the Houses of the time shouldered the blame for the plague, their families killed by rioters if the fevers hadn't reached them first. Roshan, though decimated by the plague, survived the purge. The book she perused was not clear how.

Saroya scribbled notes about other books she should look into, then packed up her papers and headed back to the castle. Her next free day wasn't for a week but she needed to be well rested and mentally prepared or her plans would fail.

∾ ∽

Saroya wiped her moist palms on her tunic and checked that she was still presentable. Then she gave the door a sharp knock. Everything hinged on appearing confident and assured. She pushed the door open at the answering "Enter!", threw back her shoulders, and strode into the room.

The three master builders studied her from behind a long table. The one in the middle, Master Dila, fingered her application. Then, glancing at his two colleagues, he set it aside.

"Mistress Bardan, I must admit I was sceptical of your qualifications. It is not often that a potential Talent first comes to our attention at your age."

Saroya stared him straight in the eye. One of his eyelids drooped. "I understand, Master. When my mother took ill, I abandoned my studies to take care of her." The easiness of the lie surprised her.

"And now that she has passed away you wish to resume your learning?"

"Yes, Master. I know I will need to work hard to catch up, but if you will just give me a chance …"

The builder on the left pursed fleshy lips. He looked as though he had spent his life building taverns and then overindulging in their wares. He cleared his throat.

"Builder Goha Ferlen is impressed with your skills. You are fortunate he felt moved to write you this letter of recommendation." He turned to his colleagues. "I see no reason to delay any longer."

Master Dila nodded. "Have your possessions delivered to the guildhall. You begin your advanced classes as soon as you are able."

Saroya wanted to rush up to him and hug him, but she only permitted herself a demure smile. She thanked the committee, bowed, and left the room, resisting the temptation to steal one final look at the letter on the table.

It wasn't until she was outside the guildhall and around the corner that she collapsed against a wall and let what had happened sink in. They had accepted the letter!

The biggest risk of her plan—and it worked! Nalini hadn't wanted to approach her family for her, so Saroya forged her own reference letter. After researching the famous Ferlen clan builders and rejecting those who were too well known, or dead, she settled on Goha Ferlen, a builder of small repute, but well respected as a teacher. He lived in Galon Ford, far enough away that she could be reasonably certain he wouldn't suddenly appear in U'Veyle. She located some of his signed plans for a tax collection office stored in a little-used section of the library. From there, it had been, while not simple, at least achievable after much practice to forge his signature.

It pained her to go behind her friend's back. Without an avenue to appeal her final Testing, Saroya couldn't see any other way to create the opportunity she needed. One small signature, in exchange for the chance to show the Adepts how wrong they were about her Untalent. Saroya felt sure Nalini would understand once she'd proven herself. Who knew? Maybe once she'd shown them all how good a builder she could be, doors would open for other Untalents too.

The Builder's Guild! Saroya took a shaky breath. No more manure duty. No mines. No more worrying if Martezha lurked around every corner. With luck, one day, a little respect might come her way. At least she'd be better positioned to research Queen Padvai and House Roshan.

She headed to the castle. She'd have to make up some explanation for her departure for Mistress Weeda. If anybody at the castle got wind of this, they would report her to the guild.

∞ ∽

Two weeks after she'd moved into the guildhall, Saroya still waited for her life to get easier. In her make up classes with the students who would receive their apprenticeships next year, the high standards daunted her. Never her strong point at the Cloister, the drafting class was her biggest nemesis. Her teacher remained less than impressed with her skills. The excuse of caring for her ailing mother would have currency for only so long before the guild became suspicious. She put all her effort into studying as hard as possible, but too often when she tried to focus on the minutiae of building, her mind presented her with some new idea. She'd come to her senses an hour later with tons of interesting off-topic doodles and notes, but no closer to finishing her current assignment.

Today, on a class field trip, the instructor pointed out the street network, linked by bridges crossing the canals and the arms of the river delta. Ditches lining the edges of roads carried rainwater and offal to the waterways. Flagstone and cobbles paved major streets. Smaller cross streets consisted of hard-packed dirt. Except for today. After the night's rain, thick mud mixed with waste sucked at Saroya's shoes. The odour made her gag. That, and the sight of the rats feasting off the trash lining the alleys. Saroya jumped sideways as a housemistress tipped a bucket out a window, the slop hitting the street with a wet splat. A wayward splash trickled coldly down Saroya's shin. She trailed after her classmates, the sight of the brown, turbid canal water reminding her not to be tempted into a swim.

They arrived at a large lake: U'Veyle's reservoir. She listened to the builder drone on about the aqueducts that fed the city its drinking water, funnelling clean rainwater into the fountains. She let herself daydream about letting go of all the worry and splashing about in a fountain herself.

"Mistress Bardan?"

Saroya stared at the instructor, nonplussed.

"You didn't even hear my question, did you? Why do we drink only from the fountains and not the underground cisterns?"

"I—uh ..." Well heads in the squares accessed

underground cisterns that also trapped rainwater runoff. For a moment she blanked.

"No self-respecting cook would use cistern water for cooking. Why?"

You know this. The skin of her shin tightened where the offal had dried. "The garbage?"

"Correct. Water, and waste, flows down." As a result, the citizens only used cistern water for washing.

Saroya wondered if aqueducts could also be used to keep the streets cleaner, while still allowing the river to make off with most of the waste. She mentally kicked herself. *You're here to study the aqueducts, dummy!* She filed away her idea for another day, when she was more established as a builder. Right now, the less attention she drew to herself, the better.

∞ ∽

Loric stifled a yawn. Enduring Urdig's new proud father routine—really, it was too much. The noble Houses of U'Veyle had each received an invitation—Loric viewed it more as a summons—to Martezha's first official function: a concert and speech at the opening of the new arboretum. He applauded desultorily as her aria drew to a close. He did not hold much of an appreciation for music, but Isolte assured him the new heir was quite good.

He took a cup of wine from a passing servant and positioned himself so that he could survey the garden and wait for his quarry to approach. It wouldn't do to appear to seek her out. He sipped the drink, and nodded politely as his glance crossed that of the head of House Maghra. The fool still had no idea that Loric was behind the man's loss of the trading rights to Ileggi grain.

Loric was feigning interest in the latest succession issues of House Biali when Martezha sashayed past. He extricated himself from the conversation and touched her arm. Martezha turned and gave him an appraising stare. He bowed, and reached for her hand. "I am remiss—I have not introduced myself yet. I am your uncle, Loric of Dorn. My wife Isolte was your mother's sister."

Martezha dipped a slight curtsy in return. He noted the precise height and had no doubt that she was fully aware of its significance with respect to their relative stature. She wasted no time learning the protocols, this one.

"A pleasure to meet you, Uncle Loric. You do not come to the castle often?"

He smiled. How aware was she of the political undercurrents of U'Veyle? He doubted she had enough experience yet to suspect his aspirations. But he resolved not to underestimate her. The wide green eyes hid a cunning mind. He had already witnessed how quickly she could snatch at opportunity when it arose.

"No, my House duties keep me away, I'm afraid. I enjoyed your delightful program for us. You are a great Talent in your field."

"An uncle who flatters—should I be wary?"

"You are adjusting well to castle life, I see. It must have been quite a shock for you at first."

"Yes, far different from Adram Vale."

"I am honoured to welcome you to the family. Whatever assistance I may provide, please feel free to ask it."

"Thank you, Uncle. I am most grateful."

"Your fellow students—how have they taken the news?"

"Oh, surprise, by and by. My friends were so happy for me."

"What of your enemies?"

"Beg pardon?"

"Some among your peers were not so pleased ... For instance, one young woman was quite upset, I gather." Martezha shot him a veiled glance, though he saw her difficulty maintaining her composure.

"I'm sure I don't know what you mean."

"Oh, come now. You have nothing to fear from me. But —given her allegations, I am surprised you have not kept a closer eye on her."

"She's a servant in the castle. How much closer could she be?"

"So you know who I mean. But you misspeak. She was a member of the castle staff, but no longer." His surveillance of the Untalent had paid off.

"Weeda kicked her out, did she?" Martezha smirked.

"I'm afraid not. I'm told she's found a place with the Builder's Guild."

Martezha shrugged. "Good riddance. Better she rot in their kitchen than mine."

"I suppose." Loric smiled and turned to go, then

swivelled back as though sharing an afterthought. "But she's not in the kitchen. The guild gave her full entry. It was a pleasure meeting you, my dear, but I must consult with Lord Garric on the state of his timber harvest. I'm sure we will be seeing much of each other."

He left her to mull over his news, but took up a station behind a screen of shrubs, where he could observe Martezha's reaction as she joined Urdig and the other officials prior to her speech.

In the heat of the day, she stood in the shade of a large oak tree. Martezha brushed away a seamstress making last minute adjustments to the hem of her dress. Urdig turned away from the scene as the buildmaster standing next to him cleared his throat. Loric could just hear them conversing.

"We are so pleased that Her Royal Highness is able to dedicate the new park," the buildmaster said. He mopped his forehead with a handkerchief. His pudgy fingers worried the corner of the cloth after he stuffed it back into his pocket. "We are ready, Majesty, if Her Highness is so disposed."

Urdig turned to fetch her.

"Martezha? It is time."

She slapped away the seamstress's hand fussing with a drape of fabric at her waist and made a moue. "My hair?"

"Lovely. Come."

"Wait! That lily." She pointed towards a bed of flowers next to the tree and waved the seamstress over again. "Sew it to my belt."

"But Highness—"

"Do it!"

"My dear, a little more graciousness towards the help would not be uncalled for," Urdig said. He continued, "They are waiting for you."

"If the jeweller you sent me had known his trade—but he didn't, and I have no decoration. The lily sets off my skin."

From his vantage point, Loric noticed her trembling hands.

Urdig must have noticed too, because he asked, "Are you all right?"

"Fine, yes. I'm fine. Just get me the flower." Martezha smoothed the irritated frown from her forehead, swallowed and took several deep breaths while the seamstress sewed the requested flower to her belt. If Loric didn't know better, he would have said she was suffering from incipient stage fright. The seamstress indicated she was done, so Martezha gave her arm to the man she now called Father. "I'm ready."

Loric followed as they made their way down the gravelled path to the open-air rotunda where the buildmaster and agronomist awaited them. A crowd of nobles bowed as the pair came into view. Martezha glided up the stairs and took her place on the dais. The buildmaster presented her with a gilded key, meant to represent the opening of the park's gates. The agronomist rolled a small cart carrying a flowering tree to a position next to her. "A gift for Her Highness."

Martezha, looking shaky, gave her prepared speech.

When it was done, Loric observed her escape to the refreshment table and sidled closer. The buildmaster offered her a glass of sparkling wine. "Highness, we are most grateful you graced us with your presence today—such an honour."

"The honour is mine, Buildmaster Dila. Your work is a credit to the realm," Martezha said. Loric felt the rotunda looked heavy and awkward. "I have a question for you," Martezha continued. Loric held his breath.

"About the rotunda, Highness? It was built with—"

"No, no, nothing to do with that. About the Builder's Guild."

"The guild? Your Highness is a musician, is she not?"

"Yes. Soon to be a full member of my guild as well. They have high entrance standards. I had thought all the guilds had such standards, but it appears I am mistaken about the Builder's Guild."

The buildmaster spluttered in confusion. "Your Highness is not happy with my work?"

Martezha rolled her eyes. "Your work is perfectly acceptable. No, I am simply puzzled by the guild's recent admission of someone I know."

The buildmaster's confusion increased. "This person is not a builder, in your esteem?"

"Since she was most recently a member of the castle's stable staff, I should think not. If I were you, I would have the guild scrutinize whatever credentials she presented."

The buildmaster looked completely taken aback. "Who is

this person, Highness?"

Martezha smiled. Loric clenched his fist in triumph.

CHAPTER 7

Elbows on the desk, Saroya kneaded her forehead, her eyes gritty with exhaustion. She knew exactly what she wanted to accomplish with her offal removal system, but she just couldn't draw it—a clean way to represent the underground network of aqueducts eluded her. Conceptually, it was simple—replace the uncovered street ditches with enclosed tunnels then add drain holes in the flagstones to catch runoff, and pipes to remove waste from homes. Small feeder pipes would lead to larger pipes debouching into major arms of the river or the open sea. The idea would go a long way to cleaning up the city streets and eliminating the odours she so hated. She stared at the sketches on her slate in frustration. None! Not one was worth transferring to parchment. She'd been up all night with nothing to show for her efforts.

A crow cawed outside; such a simple life—hunt shellfish all day, and return to the rookery every night to be surrounded by family. No worries about acceptance. No fears of being cast out. No sketches to produce for review first thing in the morning.

She would just have to explain to her drafting teacher, Master Murtag, that the inspiration had not come.

She dropped her chalk, pushed the slate away, stretched and yawned, then fetched fresh water for washing. Then she slouched off in search of some tea in the kitchens to clear her fuzzy head. On top of everything else, the guild kept her so busy her search for Veshwa was now stalled.

She stirred cream into her cup. Varzha, a fellow apprentice who'd been helping her with some of her assignments, showed up.

"How'd you make out?"

"Bah—I'm having trouble with the diagrams. Back to the drawing board, I suppose."

"I spotted Master Dila at your door before I came down. You must have just missed him."

"What could he want with me?" Aside from her required courses, she'd steered clear of Dila since her entrance interview.

"You're to report to his office after breakfast."

Saroya felt the bottom drop out of her stomach.

"Huh. I didn't think I did that badly on the materials assignment."

Varzha grinned, and raised his cup. "Better fortify yourself."

Saroya gave him a weak smile.

Master Dila's stern expression as she entered his office confirmed her worst fears. She glanced at the two other men in the room but did not recognize them. Dila came straight to the point.

"Mistress Bardan, do you recognize this person?"

Saroya peered at the man to Dila's left. She feared she knew what the correct answer was, but it would not get her far.

Dila shook his head. "No, I thought not. This is Goha Ferlen. Goha Ferlen has never met you, and never wrote a letter of reference for you. What have you to say for yourself?"

Saroya swallowed the lump in her throat and attempted to pull herself together. Her voice shook. "I apologize for deceiving you, Master Dila, but I just did not see any other way to show you what I'm capable of doing."

"Capable? You are failing half your apprenticeships. Your ideas are impractical and fanciful. We are builders here, not dreamers. How did you settle on Goha Ferlen's name to besmirch?"

Saroya could find no sympathy in any of the faces before her. "I know his family through a friend of mine," she whispered.

"Which friend?"

Saroya didn't answer. Nalini would be so angry. What would her parents say to her when they found out?

The master builder slammed his hand down on the table. "Answer me! Which friend?"

"N-Nalini Ferlen, the apprentice healer. She had nothing to do with this, I swear. She doesn't even know. Please don't punish her."

Dila's mouth set into a grim line. "She is not the one who should worry about punishment. I am fetching the magistrates. The guild cannot tolerate a fraud like this."

"But—"

"The reputations of Master Ferlen and the guild have suffered enough. Dismissed."

Saroya turned and left the room with her head held high. She refused to let them see her cowed. When she rounded the corner to the stairs, she fled to her room. Maybe if she left quickly enough, she could evade the magistrates. She crammed her meagre possessions into a saddlebag. She found a leather sheet to encase her drawings. Maybe one day they'd be useful.

Varzha walked in. "What are you doing?"

Saroya explained in as few words as possible. "I want to thank you for all your help. It meant a lot to me." She held out her hand. "I hope we can still be friends."

Varzha slapped her, hard.

"Friends? After humiliating me like this? And the guild? The sooner you're out of my sight the better."

Rubbing her stinging cheek, Saroya avoided anybody she saw in the corridors as she exited the guildhall. She trotted down the hall's stately entrance stairway, but saw no sign of the law officers. A voice behind her called her name. She pretended she had not heard—she could still escape—but the person called out again more insistently, so, turning around and laying her gear on the step beside her, she braced herself to hear out her summoner.

It was Goha Ferlen.

He trod down the last few steps towards her. Too overwhelmed in Master Dila's office, she had not taken in much of his appearance. His stature was typically Ferlen: short, with a slim build. He stooped with age, which made him appear even smaller. Nevertheless, given the circumstances, she found him imposing. He was a distant cousin to Nalini's father. He stopped on the step above her, meeting her gaze eye to eye.

"Why?"

Saroya studied the granite carving of a lion's head on the balustrade as she contemplated her answer. When she met his rheumy eyes again, she was surprised to see genuine concern in place of the censure she'd expected.

"Maybe I'll never be a builder. But I know I'm more than just a stable hand. I just need someone to believe in me." She paused, and looked over his shoulder at the builders' sigil over the doorway. "If I'd told the truth, the guild—they'd have turned me away. My ideas—they could work. I can't draw them at all, but maybe one day, if I describe them to someone like you, that person can build them for me. For everyone."

She glanced down at her feet, and took a deep breath.

"I am sorry for the trouble I've caused you. I hope you didn't come all this way just to deal with me."

He gave her a wry smile. "No. I came to U'Veyle on business and when Dila ran into me, the news of my new 'protégée' took me by surprise. Your secret might never have come out if not for a crack in the foundation of a building I designed several years ago."

"It probably would have come out once Master Murtag saw my assignment this morning."

"Perhaps. But if you read certain histories you might find that many of your kind have gone undetected in the guilds for quite a long time—sometimes lifetimes. The guilds do not like to publicize this fact. It begs the question: what is Talent, if an Untalent can feign it? Many of these supposed Untalents are responsible for great advances in their fields. They tend to be known as dabblers within their guilds."

Saroya stared at him. Not the lecture she'd expected.

"Your designs, while rough, appear quite innovative to me. I believe you could have kept your head above water for quite some time in the guild, were it not that you have an important enemy." Saroya stared at him, tense again.

"Chance did not bring your lack of Talent to the guild's attention. The princess took pains to point out your lack of qualifications to them. Why this might be of such personal concern to her, I don't understand—do you?"

Saroya swallowed. He gave her a little pat on the shoulder, then took her hand and pressed something into it —a ten-weight coin, and a small piece of parchment inscribed with his name and a street number in Galon Ford.

"If you are ever in Galon Ford, and need someone to do

those drawings for you, look me up. Give Nalini my best. I hear she's doing great things in the Healer's Guild." Before Saroya could thank him, he turned and slowly made his way back up the stairs and into the guildhall. Down the street, she spotted two official-looking men wearing the black coats of magistrates. She grabbed her bag and ran.

∞ ∞

Loric resented Daravela's summons to the Order's hall so late in the evening. Why had she insisted he bring Isolte with him?

Daravela slapped a parchment down onto the desk before her. "The Bardan girl's Testing results. The doyenne in Adram Vale did not err—there's no clear Talent here." Daravela riffled through more papers. She rubbed her temple, seemingly lost in thought. Then she fixed Isolte with a piercing stare. "What is House Roshan up to?"

"Excuse me?"

"Don't play innocent with me, my dear. Since the Great Plague, not once has your family nominated one of their own for election by the Houses to the royal throne. Not since Testing exposed the taint of Untalent in your line."

Isolte sat back, visibly flustered. Loric decided to let her flounder and see where Daravela led them. "Why is that a problem?" Isolte asked.

"Just because you're working behind the scenes doesn't mean the Order doesn't know what you're up to."

Loric thought he understood. Each time the Order

attempted to gain a seat in the Great Circle of Houses, its efforts failed. The Houses refused to relinquish their power. Especially those that had something to lose come Testing time. Loric knew of several older Houses that discreetly lobbied against the Order. They were careful to do nothing the Order could ever prove.

Daravela continued. "Don't think that Roshan's low profile will keep you from going unnoticed when the Order finally proves your family has been faking Talent certificates."

"How dare you!" Isolte cried out.

Daravela waved several parchments in Isolte's face. "I've been reviewing the records. Once every generation or two, a Roshan child's Talent emerges by a slim margin. These Talent certificates lack a second Adept examiner's signature —Queen Padvai's certificate included!"

"I know nothing of this. It would be my father's doing if anything. Surely you're not implying that my own certificate —"

"No. But if we could find a way to tie this conspiracy to Urdig ..."

With mounting excitement, Loric stared at Isolte. "Did he know when he married Padvai that the certificate was a fake?"

Isolte shrugged. "It would be hard to prove."

"I have another question," Daravela said. "If your family found a way to bribe Adepts into certifying their Untalents, why did Padvai hide the Bardan girl?"

∞ ∽

"How could you?"

Saroya didn't have an answer to Nalini's question. They sat in the garden of the Healer's Guild. Saroya had decided it would be best to spill the sorry tale of her brief foray into the Builder's Guild to Nalini before some other offended Ferlen got to her first.

"I'm sorry, Nalini. I didn't think it would hurt anyone. I know it was wrong, but—"

"This is my family's name we're talking about. You've made a laughing stock of Ferlens everywhere."

"Nobody's laughing, believe me." Saroya wondered how being laughed at could be worse than how people treated her.

"Why would anyone believe anything you say anymore?"

"Nalini—"

"Give me one reason why I should still be your friend."

"Even Goha Ferlen wasn't as angry as you are."

"If he's willing to forgive you, it's not to your credit."

Through her shame, Saroya repressed a surge of indignation. She'd apologized, hadn't she? Why couldn't Nalini see? See how hard life was for her? "It's not like I stole from him."

"Stealing isn't just about money. You stole my name. You stole his. Just because you don't have a family doesn't mean you can get away with disrespecting mine."

"But they don't even respect you."

Nalini sat back as if Saroya had slapped her.

"I love my parents. My sister warned me to cut you out of my life a while ago, but I thought I should give you a break."

"Oh, so now I'm some pity case, is that it?"

"I could put up with a lot from you but not lies. And certainly not taking advantage of the people I love behind my back."

"But—"

"Get out." Nalini stood and pointed at the door. Saroya left. She regretted her words, but there was no taking them back. How had her apology spiralled down into such bitterness? Who was she angrier with: Nalini or herself?

∞ ∞

Saroya parlayed the funds from Goha Ferlen's small gift into a dingy lodging above a tanner's shop. With the rent due weekly, she needed to find a paying wage within the next two weeks if she wanted to stay off the streets.

She relentlessly canvassed the neighbourhood, but none of the tradespeople would take her on without a recommendation from a guild. She had no luck convincing any of the small, family-owned shops that she could add to their business. She stopped telling potential employers about her stint at the castle; when she could not provide a reasonable excuse for leaving such a plum assignment, their interest turned to suspicion. Every night she returned to her tiny room footsore and discouraged, her nose wrinkling at the nauseating smell from the tanning vats. Her remaining coins dwindled and she rationed her food intake. Her stomach growled in protest.

Shop owners chased her out with foul language and once even a thrown shoe when they discovered she was Untalented. The only person who'd been even somewhat encouraging, a scribe, gave her a sheet of calligraphy samples. "Come back in two years if you've mastered all the forms," he said. Like that would help her now.

On this particular cloudy morning she roused herself out of bed with little enthusiasm. Though she tiptoed down the rickety staircase, the landlord pounced on her at the bottom.

"Rent's due tomorrow."

"Then don't bother me 'til then," Saroya said.

The skinny man eyed her pouch doubtfully. "Don't look like that holds enough coin."

"Only fools carry all their money with them." She wanted to take back the remark as soon as it came out; he'd probably search her room now looking for a stash. Not that he'd find anything.

Saroya pushed past him and headed for a fruitmonger. She picked out a bruised apple and, pointing out the blemish, haggled down the price.

At the end of the street, a magistrate rounded the corner. Were they still looking for her? She ducked into a dark, narrow tunnel underneath the second floor of two buildings. The hidden alley opened out into a courtyard bordered on its far side by a narrow canal. Across the water, the pink splash of geraniums spilled over the low wall of an enclosed garden. They gave her something pretty to stare at, her feet dabbling at the canal water lapping against the stone.

She tallied in her head her short list of friends. In time Nalini might forgive Saroya but time was not a luxury she possessed. Saroya could expect little enthusiasm from Mistress Weeda or Master Guffin for a return to castle service. Not that being anywhere near Martezha seemed wise. None of the Adram Vale students would give her the time of day. Oddly enough, Goha Ferlen best understood her predicament. But he had already gone back to Galon Ford. She needed help, and she needed it soon.

Her thoughts turned to Eiden Callor. Even though he disbelieved her story, she still felt he was responsible for getting her the work with Master Guffin. She doubted Callor would see her but there was no harm in trying.

The watchman rebuffed her on sight when she approached the officers' quarters; what possible business could someone dressed like she was have with the captain of the King's Guards? Finally, she convinced him to bring Callor a note. She waited in the spartan hallway, avoiding the stares of curious soldiers, for over half an hour.

A door opened across from the lounge and an aide beckoned to her. She followed him into the room. Two battle-axes hung crossed over the door, and maps of the kingdom lined the walls. The ornate crest of the King's Guards inlaid into the granite floor reinforced that she came as a petitioner. The aide motioned at an inner door then retired to his desk in the anteroom.

Crossing the threshold into Callor's office, Saroya squinted at the glare from the window. Callor stood silhouetted behind the desk. He did not come forward to greet her and she could not make out his expression. She stopped a few feet from the desk, not knowing how to begin. His continuing silence made her feel more and more like a supplicant. She needed him to think well of her, yet what she came to ask would lower his opinion of her. Sensing his impatience, she cleared her throat.

"Captain Callor, thank you so much for agreeing to see me."

"Please get to the point." His chilly tone discouraged her even further.

"I need work," she blurted, then felt her cheeks colouring.

"I went to some lengths to get you a perfectly decent position at the castle. You could not hope for much better, yet you threw out the opportunity like so many dinner leavings."

Saroya looked at her feet. "It was stupid and ungrateful of me to leave the castle, yes. But I wasn't ready to give up on finding ... some thing, some way of making my own mark on the world." She searched out his eyes but the sunlight pouring in the window behind him stymied her. "Surely you can understand this."

"And now you are ready? To give up?"

No, but how to explain? She needed to eat. "No one will

have me. I've tried, and tried." Her voice shook as all the humiliations of the past month pushed through. "I'll take anything." She could taste the sourness of those words. "Anything, as long as it's not here at the castle."

"Why come to me? And why not the castle?"

She swallowed. "Because you know the city better than anybody else I know. Everyone from Adram Vale has disappeared into their guilds, and even the ones who don't despise me are too busy to help."

"You haven't answered my second question."

"Martezha—I mean, Her Highness—she and I, we don't … she doesn't …" Resignation tinged Saroya's smile. "She would rather not be reminded I exist."

She fidgeted with a strand of hair. She sensed Callor come to some decision, and held her breath.

"Those who leave their stamp upon history and the world don't give up at the first setback. Leave me now. See Mistress Weeda on your way out—she has a letter for you."

She had been judged and found wanting.

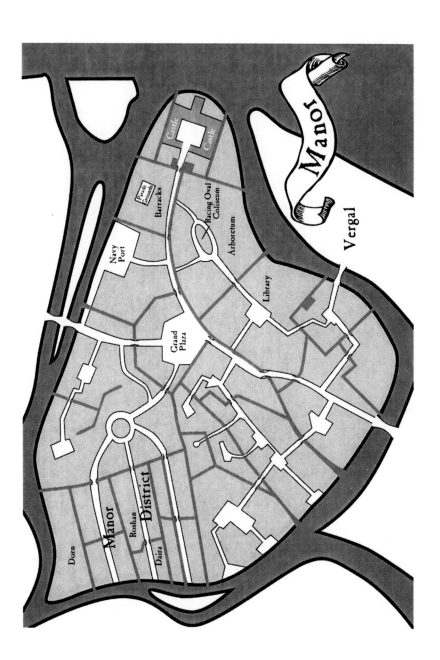

CHAPTER 8

The cold knot of desperation tightened in Saroya's chest. It had been growing since the initial numbness after her meeting with Eiden Callor wore off. Many times since then, she'd examined herself with his eyes and did not like the view.

Worse, the parchment handed to her by a stern-mouthed Mistress Weeda proved to be the long-awaited reply from the doyenne in Adram Vale. Its contents had not lived up to her expectations. Of the note and ring, none could remember.

Saroya checked her coin pouch—empty. Her stomach gurgled, just as empty. She looked around the small room. It wasn't much, but with the rent overdue, it was no longer hers. She reached for the latch on her way out again, but a sharp rap on the door made her flinch. She snatched her hand back as if the hasp had burned her. Surely she was not being kicked out of the room now? So stupid not to slip out unnoticed.

The weasel-like face of her landlord greeted her when she opened the door.

"Pay up. That's three days you owe me."

"I don't have the money."

He grabbed her arm. "I don't run an almshouse. Pay up or I'll bond you. You can work off what you owe."

Indenture! Saroya swallowed. How could she possibly lose her freedom over three days' rent?

The landlord dragged her roughly down the stairs, and Saroya panicked. Tales flashed through her head of people bonded over minor debts remaining indentured for years, slaves of their owners. She couldn't let this happen! He yanked her out the door into the darkening street. She tripped and fell, breaking his grip. He snarled and lunged for her, but she scrambled up. She took off running.

"Stop her!"

A passerby tried to get in her way but she darted around him, the landlord hot on her heels. She could hear him wheezing for breath. She picked up speed, aiming for the maze of streets around Market Square. The black coat of a magistrate loomed before her. Saroya veered left into an alley. She careened through a tiny square surrounded by dingy buildings. Footsteps pounded behind her. At the far end of the square, she slid to a stop. Buildings loomed on two sides, and canal waters lapped at her feet. Saroya peered back the way she had come but the landlord and a magistrate blocked the alley. Cornered! Without thinking, Saroya dove into the canal.

∞ ∽

Loric took a cup of wine from the steward. He ignored the vapid chatter of the woman seated to his right, instead watching the activity at the head of the table. Dinner drew to a close, and his anticipation mounted. It was always entertaining to watch someone squirm.

Urdig stood and bid his guests to join him on the large balcony outside the Great Hall. The lantern procession was to begin in the castle gardens and wind its way throughout the city, followed by jugglers, dancers, stilt walkers and other entertainment. The winter rains had abated for a few days and the evening was fine, the air crisp—just in time for the solstice festivities. Frost would blanket the ground in the morning.

While the guests rose and made their way outdoors, servants draping warm cloaks across their backs, Loric insinuated himself behind Princess Martezha. They passed a doorway, and he pressed his hand into the small of her back, leaned across and redirected her into a small drawing room. A final glance down the hall confirmed that Isolte still distracted Urdig with small talk.

Martezha rounded on him, in a hurry to exit the room, but Loric stood firm against the door.

"What do you mean by this?"

"You would deny your uncle a quick chat with his favourite niece?"

"Make it quick—I was looking forward to the procession."

Loric sidled away from the door, and took a languorous sip of wine, knowing this would annoy her more.

"My brother-in-law is a trusting man." He smirked. "Too trusting, do you not agree?"

Martezha stiffened. "I don't understand."

"I think you do. My emissary returned from Tarash just before the passes closed for the winter. He brought some interesting news regarding a couple by the name of Baghore." He savoured another sip of wine. It tasted almost as good as the expression on Martezha's face. "My dear, you look unwell. Why don't you sit down?"

Martezha dropped into the chair next to her, not bothering to arrange her skirts. Loric sank onto a neighbouring settee, crossed his legs and admired his leather boots. "Would you like me to tell you their story?"

Martezha shook her head slightly.

"You know it then, do you?" Her venomous stare only amused him more. "I think it's worth repeating nonetheless."

In the distance, he heard the processional drumbeats strike up. He tapped his foot idly in time. "An indentured Untalented couple, each springing from a long line of similar unfortunates, with no money to their name, find themselves expecting a child. With no means to support a family, the costs of feeding a child will keep them indentured even longer. They abandon the baby with the Adepts of Adram Vale, leaving nothing else but a note giving her name." He swirled the dregs of his wine around the bottom of the goblet. "Lucky for me, they left their real surname, which my man tracked back to them. Less lucky for you."

"What do you want?"

"Nothing—for now. It suits me to leave you where you are."

Martezha shrugged. "If you've found me out, it's only a matter of time before someone else does. That Callor man seems suspicious."

"He sent his own man back to Adram Vale when you arrived at the castle. Mine got there first. The Cloister's records have been purged, appropriate people paid to forget, and I've personally assumed your parents' bond and bundled them off to my estate south of the city, where they can speak to no one. Your position is secure for as long as I need it to be."

"You must want something in return."

"Most certainly, my sweet. You are uniquely placed to grant me certain favours. A word in Urdig's ear … A well-timed suggestion. You need do nothing more difficult than that."

Martezha marshalled the remains of her dignity. "Fine. We will not speak of this again." She swept from the room, but Loric noticed the tremor in her fingers as she fumbled to open the door.

∾ ∽

Saroya clung shivering to a piling, two buildings down

and across from the square where she dove into the water. The magistrate had left the landlord in the square to prevent her from climbing out there. The lawman peered into the water from the bridge one hundred paces away. She didn't think he could see her, but she was trapped between the two men.

Her feet had already gone numb, and her forehead tightened from the headache that blossomed as soon as she sliced through the water. Her heart skipped erratically at the shock of the cold. If she didn't find a way out soon, she'd freeze.

The dark shape of a barge nosed out from underneath the bridge in the deepening evening gloom. It passed the pilings. There! A line trailed from the side closest to her, opposite from where the bargemaster stood. She pushed off the pilings and grabbed the rope. Unaware he'd hooked a stowaway, the bargemaster poled his craft along the canal. They floated past the square, Saroya hidden from the landlord's view.

Three bridges further, Saroya's fingers refused to grip the rope any longer. It slipped from her grasp, and she floundered to the edge of the canal and hauled herself out. She spat onto the cobbles, in a vain effort to clear the sour taste of the canal from her mouth.

She spent the night huddled in the corner of an empty stable, teeth chattering. She hung her sopping clothes to dry and wrapped herself in an old horse blanket. She snuck out before dawn in search of a washhouse, her skin shrinking away from her damp clothes. She waited until the laundry filled with women then with everyone occupied by their washing, she plucked a cloak and tunic from the drying lines. Reduced to stealing. She shrugged off the shame. She wouldn't survive the winter without a cloak.

That afternoon, the temperature warmed as clouds shrouded the sky. The cold snap over, a light drizzle varnished the cobbles. Saroya squatted underneath a large willow, rain dripping from her hood as she stared at the gates of House Roshan. She might be homeless but she no longer had an excuse to put off the search for the mysterious Veshwa mentioned in the note. Did Veshwa still serve her mother's maiden House? There was only one way to find out —sneak inside Manor Roshan.

Two riders trotted up the drive. Saroya overheard a snatch of conversation as they went by.

"… wine for the party tonight," the man on the chestnut mare said.

"I won't hear the end of it from Lady Kasturi if we come back empty-handed," his companion answered.

Party? Maybe this was the opening she needed. Saroya stretched her cramped legs and slipped away into the drizzle.

Two hours later she knocked on the door of a nondescript building just off the Grand Plaza. Nothing marked it out as special except the castle sigil carved into the stone doorframe—this was the fitter's, where she had come so long ago to have her castle livery tailored. The woman who answered took one look at Saroya's threadbare clothing and tried to shut the door in her face.

"Wait!" Saroya said. "You know me—you fit me for stable livery. Mistress Weeda sent me?"

The woman peered at Saroya. Recognition dawned in her eyes. "What are you doing looking like a drowned rat? Weeda runs a tighter ship than this."

Saroya tried to look sheepish. "I have a problem—all my tunics are with the laundress. I put on my only clean one this morning. Then I fell in the muck while cleaning out a stall. Mistress Weeda will kill me. I'm supposed to be footman for the coach taking the princess to the House Roshan party tonight. If I'm not presentable—"

"Enough, child. I know what it's like being on Weeda's bad side. Let me see what I have."

Saroya marched out the door with a large bundle slung over her shoulder. She'd told the fitter she wanted to keep the new clothes clean until this evening. She told herself taking castle livery didn't count as stealing. Not when everything in the castle belonged to her own father.

That evening, she again crouched beneath the shelter of the willow, studying the coaches as they entered the gates of House Roshan with passengers bound for the party. Each coach sported a full complement of drivers and footmen. Her stomach knotted. She had to get in!

A polished coach with a minor House sigil rolled up the street, curtains drawn. It passed the willow, Saroya noting the lone driver. No footman sat on the transom! While the gate guard conversed with the driver, Saroya darted out of her hiding place until she stood at the rear of the carriage, timing her leap into the transom seat with the lurch of the carriage starting forward. The coach rumbled past the gate guard, and Saroya gave him a friendly wave. Halfway up the drive, she jumped off the carriage and slipped into the trees.

Arriving coaches crowded the gravel driveway, while shiny black barques disgorged passengers onto the estate's canal promenade. Guests arriving by water approached the house via a pathway sheltered by climbing vines. Saroya snuck up to the side of the stables then strolled up to the servants' entrance as though she had every right to be there. A houseboy didn't give her livery a second glance before leading her off to the back of the house.

As many servants as guests clustered in the back rooms of the mansion. The houseboy left Saroya in a small parlour. "Stay away from the kitchens," he warned, pointing to the servants scurrying to and fro with heaping trays of food for the party. "Cook's assistant just smashed into some numbskull page from House Tikla. What a disaster." The wails of the cook—"Just look what you've done! The cherry tarts, the gingerbread, and oh! My candied flowers ... All ruined!"—could be heard all the way into the parlour.

The gossip and tales of infidelity among the noble Houses soon bored Saroya. She wandered over to the sideboard and poured a cup of cider from a pitcher then grabbed a pastry. Her stomach growling, she stashed two buns in her belt pouch then picked her way across the now crowded room and set off to explore the mansion.

She prowled down corridors, avoiding areas where the party roared in full swing. She didn't need to get commandeered by a noble into some irrelevant task. She climbed a dimly lit stairwell to the second floor. The landing provided the servants with access to the family's bedrooms. She did not want to be accused of pilfering any valuables, so she continued up the now narrower and steeper stairs to the third floor and the servants' quarters. A cramped hallway lined with doors spanned the whole wing. The ceiling of the room facing her sloped underneath the eaves. She tiptoed down the hall, peering into open doorways but coming across only empty rooms.

Despairing that she might not find anything, she heard a faint voice from behind a closed door. She eased the door open and peered inside.

∞ ∽

Loric held forth to the men clustered in a secluded alcove of House Roshan's reception hall. This was the most receptive group he'd addressed all evening.

"We let these people run loose. Who knows what mischief they're causing? Uneducated, desperate for money. Just the other day, the prison warden told me they amounted to over half his inmates."

"Surely you're not suggesting a central registry of Untalents, Lord Dorn."

And he hadn't even had to say a thing. "I don't know that I would have gone that far, Lord Tikla, but now that you mention it ..."

Another nobleman broke in. "My groundsman caught two of them breaking into the smokehouse. With a registry, we could have tracked them down after they hared off."

Tikla sputtered. "Enough with this registry business! I suggested no such thing. How do you even know they were Untalented?"

"They were layabouts. That sort usually is."

Loric left the alcove in search of more refreshment, and fresh terrain to plant suspicions among the noble Houses. If only he could find a serious calamity for which Untalents could be blamed. Behind him, he heard the argument grow more heated.

∞ ∾

Saroya blinked as her eyes adjusted to the extra light cast by several candles. Seated on a rocking chair in the far corner of the room, an old woman gazed back at her. A large swatch of needlework lay spread on her lap.

"Come to bring the old lady a drink?" Saroya remembered the cup of cider she held. She offered it to the woman but a gnarled hand waved it away. Saroya marvelled that the swollen knuckles were still limber enough to do such intricate sewing.

"At my age, dear, if I have a sip now, it will pass through me at a most inconvenient time of night." The corners of the woman's black eyes crinkled. "And who might you be, child? I may be old but I'm not blind yet—those aren't

Roshan colours you're wearing. Karan, if I'm not mistaken."

Saroya introduced herself. "I came up here hoping to find someone to talk to who wasn't up to their neck with party work."

"Yes, well, old Kimila's not as spry as she used to be. Still handy with the needle, but I'm as likely to drop a tray as offend one of the guests with my wrinkles. Her Ladyship prefers I stay put on nights like these. What of you? Shouldn't your neck be just as swamped by party tasks as everybody else's?"

"I have a few minutes, I think."

"Not just up here for a bit of gossip, then, are you?"

"Not really. At least, not current gossip. I'm looking for a woman called Veshwa. At least, I think she's a woman—she might have worked for House Roshan a long time ago—I'm not sure."

Kimila's coal eyes narrowed. "And what business do you have with this maybe-woman Veshwa?"

Saroya wondered how much truth to tell. "She's the only link I have to my mother."

"And your mother is?"

"Dead."

Kimila pursed her lips and frowned. The tap-tap of a tree branch knocked against the shutters. Kimila's silent scrutiny lengthened.

Saroya took her second plunge of the week. "As a baby, I was left at an orphanage with a note from my mother. It said to look for Veshwa if I ever came to U'Veyle."

136 ~ KATRINA ARCHER

"Why House Roshan?"

"The note implied she was a servant here." Saroya stretched the truth a bit.

"Are you an Untalent, then?"

Deception was pointless. Kimila's eyes seemed practiced at ferreting out lies. "Yes."

Oddly, this decided Kimila. She sighed and laid her needlework on the small table beside her.

"Veshwa. Now there's a name I haven't heard in many a year. Came to the House with Lady Ashra as part of her dowry when she married Lord Roshan. Not the current one —I mean his father, Airic of Roshan." A dreamy twinkle flickered across the jet eyes. "Now there was a wedding to behold."

Saroya stifled an impatient remark; she sensed it wouldn't do to hurry Kimila.

As though reading her thoughts, Kimila snorted. "Don't worry, dear, I'll get to the point. You'd do well to work on your gambling face though—everything you think flits across it for all to see." She closed her eyes as though cataloguing her memories.

"Veshwa arrived the year little Dhilain was born—not so little now, I suppose, seeing as he's lord of the manor. She was nursemaid and nanny to all of Ashra's children. Padvai was her favourite. Always getting into trouble, that one. Veshwa indulged her. But when Airic gave Padvai to Lord Urdig as his wife, Veshwa went to Dhilain, taking care of his children." Kimila paused, then said more softly, "That really stuck in Isolte's craw—that her sister went to House Karan. Isolte couldn't stand making an inferior match to her sister's. Then again, who could have known that Dorn would waste his Talent in that way?" Kimila shrugged, and gazed out the window. She acted like Saroya should know what she was talking about.

"A few years after the Houses crowned Urdig and they moved to the castle, Padvai summered in the lake country. She begged Dhilain to borrow Veshwa. I lost track of her after that. Don't rightly know what happened, but I heard rumours—Veshwa left in some disgrace, went to live in the Vergal Quarter." Kimila's lined face turned to Saroya. "That's all I can tell you."

Saroya knelt down and took one of Kimila's knobby hands in her own. "It's enough—you can't know how grateful I am." Her mind churned over these revelations. Disgrace. Would an illicit pregnancy qualify as disgrace? Despite the evidence of the ring, could Veshwa be her mother and not Padvai? The ring might have been doubly stolen—first by Veshwa, then by Martezha.

Kimila smiled. "Better get back, now. You'll catch trouble if anybody finds you up here." Saroya turned to go. "And girl—" Saroya looked back. "Even Untalents can do well for themselves in this world. Don't let nobody tell you otherwise." Saroya met the opaque gaze levelled at her and, though puzzled, nodded. No matter how wrong the old woman might be about Untalents, Saroya had to believe she was telling the truth about Veshwa.

∾ ∽

Orjen, the port captain, frowned at the newly arrived ship—the only vessel from the king's trade delegation to Kurtya that had returned. His irritation was not due to the loss of four ships. He marched up the gangplank, prepared to give the ship's master an earful, but stopped in puzzlement when no one greeted him at the top.

He peered towards the stern, looking for the sailors who had tossed the mooring lines ashore. At first, he saw nothing. Then, squinting at the bow, he spotted a man slumped against the strakes. His heart beating faster, he went forward, but still halted a good distance away.

"You, there!" The sailor turned his head with obvious effort. The port captain could clearly see the sheen of perspiration on the crewman's forehead. It was a cool day. Orjen swallowed.

"Why has this ship come to the docks without clearance first? Where is the master?"

The sailor licked dry, cracked lips. "Dead. The master is dead."

"Dead of what?"

"The fever. The fever got him. Please. Bring healers. We need healers."

Orjen backed away. "You fools. Do you know what you've done?" He hurried back to the top of the gangplank. He held out a hand in warning to the customs inspectors preparing to board.

"This ship is under quarantine effective immediately." He looked around for his assistant. "Bring food and water, send for a healer, and notify the castle. I need two guards posted here at the docks—and get this gangplank removed. Now! No one is to board or leave the ship." He glanced forward, his expression grim. "I'll find out if anybody already has."

His assistant bustled away, fully aware that with Orjen stuck on the ship, he was now the acting port captain. Orjen went to find himself a comfortable place aboard to await his fate.

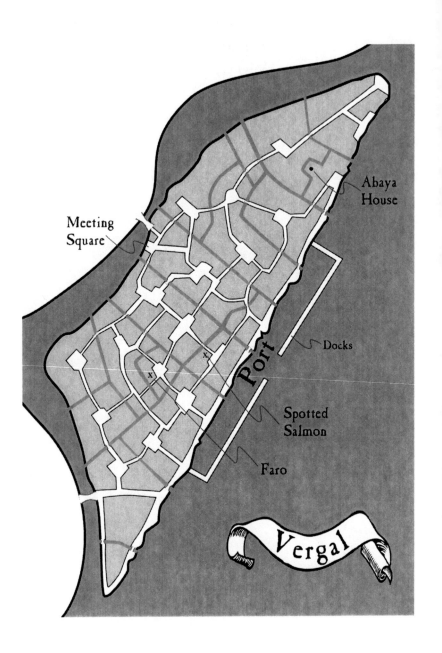

CHAPTER 9

Saroya picked herself up out of the muddy puddle and dodged a kick.

"Mine!" her attacker shouted.

She held her hands up palms out and slowly backed away. The filthy beggar who'd shoved her from behind shook his fist at her.

"My corner! My pile! Go away!"

Saroya stared wistfully at the pile of trash she'd been combing through in hopes of finding a stale crust of bread, overripe apple, or a trinket she could pawn at the market.

The beggar glowered. What scared Saroya the most about him wasn't his fierce territoriality, but his eyes. Despite the brief glow of rage when he discovered her, they exhibited nothing but defeat. No curiosity. No spark of animation. No interest in the rest of the world. Saroya didn't recognize herself in those eyes, refused to.

This man had no friends, no family to turn to for help.

His Untalent condemned him not only to destitution, but to a life of solitude. Saroya had a friend. A friend she'd betrayed. But maybe she could heal that rift. With Kimila's information, maybe she could find Veshwa. And through Veshwa, family. A place to belong.

Saroya spun on her heels and took off in search of a washhouse that wouldn't bar her entry on sight so she could clean off the mud clinging to her tunic. Running down the street, she chanted over and over.

"Not me. That's not me. It'll never be me. Not me …"

∞ ∞

Saroya waited nervously in the atrium of the Healer's Guild. The boy sent to fetch Nalini had not returned. Saroya had ruined her one friendship and where did it get her? Nowhere. Begging Nalini for forgiveness seemed a small price to pay to salvage their friendship. She would admit to Nalini how much she'd wronged her. Nalini might never understand Saroya but at least she listened. At the sound of approaching footsteps, Saroya lifted her head. Nalini stood before her.

Saroya searched her face for some sign of welcome, but Nalini stayed silent and stony. Saroya held out a small pouch.

"I found this Mourner's Veil in the market and thought you might like some. I didn't think it grew in the gardens here."

Nalini ignored the pouch. She folded her arms across her chest.

Saroya sighed. "Look, I know what I did to Goha didn't help you with your parents. I couldn't stay in the castle anymore. I didn't know what else to do." Saroya stood up, leaving the pouch on the bench she'd just vacated. "Keep the herbs; they'll help someone feel better." With a last forlorn look at Nalini, Saroya headed for the door.

Something hit Saroya in the shoulder and she spun around. The herb pouch lay at her feet. Saroya winced at the strength of Nalini's anger.

"I could use some help carrying it to my room," Nalini said. "I've got a stack of books to pick up from the library along the way."

Saroya gaped.

Nalini grinned. "Don't worry. I'm still sore at you. But Goha wrote how impressed he was by how far you got. He smoothed things over with my parents. Come on, we never finished the full tour last time."

Saroya felt like she was walking on air as they set off down the hall.

Saroya enjoyed her tour of the guildhall. While the infirmary sick rooms were off-limits due to the presence of patients, she noted that many healers still worked in their studies. The conservatory impressed her the most: all those special plants, each with its own use for treating injury or illness. Saroya didn't think it possible for a single person to remember all their names, but Nalini had to know the entire catalogue of the conservatory before her guildmaster would allow her to move past apprenticeship.

They neared the atrium again, rounded a corner and encountered a knot of healers, heads bent together in animated discussion. Their conversation cut off when they noticed the two friends. Saroya was conscious of their eyes following them as they passed the group, then the muttering resumed as the girls moved out of earshot.

"What was that all about?"

"I think the guild is worried about a ship that came in a week or two ago. The sailors were all sick, and the healers don't believe they followed the proper quarantine measures. I've heard of reports of fevers in and around the port, in the Vergal Quarter."

"But why were they so secretive?"

"They don't want to start a panic. The last time whispers of plague surfaced, the Vergal and other poor quarters rioted. More people died from the rioting than from fever." Nalini stopped, and shot her a concerned look. "You won't tell anybody about this will you? If it gets out and gets back to me, I'll have some explaining to do."

"Don't worry. Just promise me that if it really is plague, you'll give me some warning. And some special herbs." Saroya grinned. "You said the Vergal?"

"Yes. The usual fanatics are saying the Vergalers brought it on themselves with their lifestyles, but I think there's some other reason why the fever spreads so quickly in those quarters."

"Are you going down there at all to help with the sick?" Saroya explained about Veshwa. "If so, could you ask around after Veshwa? It would mean a lot to me."

Nalini grinned. "If it means showing Martezha for the lying priss she is, I'm in. We could even go together. I'll send you a message if I go."

Saroya didn't want to admit to Nalini that she was living underneath a bridge—the only dry shelter she'd found where she didn't run the risk of being discovered and hauled before a magistrate.

"Why don't I drop by on my free day instead?" Saroya suggested. Technically every day was now a free day but there was no way she'd tell Nalini. Though Saroya had gone on forays into the Vergal, finding food and earning a few pennies begging or cleaning trash kept her too busy to go more than once or twice a week. "How bad is this plague? Would Veshwa be in danger from it if she's down in the Vergal?"

"I don't know. It depends: on how strong she is compared to the virulence of the fever."

"She's probably about your grandmother's age. Great—just when I get a lead on her location, and now this." Saroya's spirits sank.

∞ ∽

Saroya woke up worried. Increasingly dire news of fevers rattled the city, with most of the deaths reported in the heart of the Vergal. Rumours abounded, making the separation of fact from fearmongering difficult. Clearly, the illness was spreading, and fast. What if Veshwa died?

Saroya brushed bits of dirt off her tunic, and folded the frayed horse blanket she'd pilfered from the abandoned stable that first lonely night. She tucked her few belongings underneath the oilskin the fitter gave her for the purloined livery. She wedged the bundle as far underneath the bridge arch as she could. Peeking out from below the bridge, she made sure nobody was in sight before crawling out into the street. She trotted off to the Healer's Guild to fetch Nalini.

"Ready for an exploratory mission?" Saroya asked.

Nalini nodded and threw her an apple she'd swiped from the guild refectory. Saroya bit into it with relish. She'd forgotten the last time her stomach was full. Her friend looked glum.

"What's the matter, Nalini?"

"My parents are in town."

"Have they finally admitted you're a healer?"

Nalini shook her head. "They've come to get my sister settled with the Builder's Guild. They rented apartments overlooking the guild so they can take care of her while she apprentices."

"At least they're not in your hair."

They left the busy streets of the Market District, catching a small passenger barque. The barquier crossed an arm of the river, arriving at the outer island known locally as the Vergal, then took them through narrower waterways until the foul, murky canal they followed opened onto the port. Their driver deposited them with a grunt, in a hurry to get back to more lucrative routes.

Saroya and Nalini looked around a disused quay. Saroya had expected a bustling port. Instead, a large wooden crane hung out over the water, no cargo slung in its net. Only one ship floated at its mooring three slips down, without a single longshoreman in sight.

"Where is everybody?" Saroya asked.

"The port captain quarantined all arriving ships." Nalini pointed to a small island offshore. A cluster of boats anchored in a small bay.

Nalini rummaged in her belt pouch. She pulled out two triangles of cloth and handed one to Saroya. "Put this on."

Saroya followed Nalini's lead and tied the kerchief around her head so that it covered her nose and mouth. "What's it for?"

"Some of the healers think something in the air is sickening people. Have you smelled the Vergal?" Nalini feigned a gag. "Maybe if we don't breathe in the scent, we won't catch the fever."

Saroya hadn't even considered the danger to herself. The thin cloth against her nose warmed and grew damp as she let out a harsh breath. At this point, one more worry did not make much difference.

"Where to first?" Saroya asked

"The guild is trying to find some way to stop the spread, so I'd like to learn who's not sick. Why don't we wander around and look for a market? Some stall minder might know all the local gossip."

Saroya was glad for Nalini's company. The last time she

explored the Vergal, she had come at it from the opposite side. The scruffy inhabitants dressed colourfully. Saroya found their easy manner engaging. She felt safe even though the occasional shady character lurked on a street corner or skulked down an alley. This time, the lurkers and skulkers were the only people out and about. The quarter seemed as though it listened for some unheard signal. Should someone accost them, would anybody investigate their screams?

They rounded a corner and entered an empty market square. A few stall keepers desultorily displayed their wares.

"How do they make any money without customers?" Saroya asked.

"Ain't that the question, now, sweetie." The scrawny woman in the doorway spat onto the cobbles.

"Is everybody sick?" Nalini wondered.

"Sick? Nah. There's just no goods to sell, so nothing to buy, so them's that ain't sick are stayin' home. Nothin' to do but wait."

"Have you lived here long?" Saroya eyed the woman's lined countenance and didn't doubt the answer.

"Goin' on twenty years now. Can't say as they's been the best years of me life."

"Have you ever heard of a woman called Veshwa?"

"Can't say as I have. If ye're looking for someone, though, Balreg be the best person to talk to. Biggest gossip in the city, that one. Knows what colour underwear the king put on this morning, or so's he claims."

"Where can we find him?"

"He runs the Spotted Salmon Pub down on Port Street."

They spoke to a few other bored shopkeepers as they made their way through the market, and the answer was the same: business was bad, none had heard of Veshwa, and the Spotted Salmon Pub was the place to ask questions.

A drunken fishmonger, teetering over his smelly wares, gave them directions. They encountered several healers going door to door, looking for the ill. Nalini conferred briefly with each of them. In a dead-end lane they entered by accident, they saw their first body. Someone had dumped it between two row houses, well clear of either doorway. "Look," Nalini pointed out the swellings underneath the skin, "Definitely a plague victim. Her family's probably too afraid to live with the corpse." To ease her fear, Saroya tried not to think of it as a person, then felt guilty. What if it had been Veshwa? How would she feel then? Nalini sent the next healer they saw to look into proper disposal and to check for other victims.

After losing themselves in a warren of tiny streets and alleys, they spotted a landmark—a grain warehouse next to a glass-blower's. The sound of raised voices greeted them as they turned a last corner.

With some relief, Saroya noted the sign of the Spotted Salmon Pub. An unruly knot of people surrounded a man who had just left the entrance of the establishment. Approaching, Saroya and Nalini heard angry shouts.

"If that port doesn't reopen soon, I'll go out of business."

"What right do you have to play with our livelihoods like this?"

"We have mouths to feed at home."

The man at the centre of the controversy raised his hands in a call for calm. Angry mutters continued.

"Until the fever is under control, I have a responsibility to check all ships, entering or leaving, for signs of the disease. If you don't like it, take it up with King Urdig, but I think you'll find he agrees with my position."

The man, evidently a high-ranking port official, strode through the crowd and down the street. A few desperate stragglers trailed after him.

"He must be the new port captain," Nalini whispered. "I heard the other one was one of the first stricken by this plague. I should go find the new one later; maybe he has some insights into how it spreads."

"He's not a healer, Nalini."

"But he was here when it started. He knows who got sick first."

"Let's find Balreg."

They entered the pub, which did not leave much of a first impression. Tables scattered with crumbs and puddled with spilled drink were strewn about one dingy common room. Long tables lined each wall. The man tending bar behind a scratched and gouged counter did not dispel the air of seediness that hung about the place. Greasy hair fell in dank clumps about his face. He whistled through a gap in his grin where he was missing a tooth as they walked up to the bar

"And what can I get two such fine young ladies?"

"We're not here to drink," Nalini said.

He eyed them speculatively. "Didn't think so. You don't look like my usual clientele."

Saroya spoke up. "My friend here is a healer, come to help with the plague."

"We're all saved, I'm sure." Nalini frowned but Balreg looked at Saroya. "And you?"

"I'm looking for a family friend. She moved to the Vergal and we lost track of her."

"And someone told you Balreg knows everybody in the Vergal?"

"That's right."

"Did they also tell you my information doesn't come cheap?"

Saroya glanced at Nalini. "I don't have much money."

"Then I can't help you. Unless you've got other information to trade?" He gave Nalini a significant look. "Information that could help me weather the plague?"

Nalini shook her head.

"Then all I can do is offer you an ale. Come back when you have something for me."

Saroya cursed to herself. Balreg didn't look like the type of man who succumbed to pleading. She'd never make enough money to pay him, not if she couldn't even feed herself. How would she find Veshwa now?

∾ ↄ

Loric studied Martezha. Playing the solicitous aunt, Isolte had invited her to Manor Dorn for tea and on impulse asked her to perform for her guests. Martezha had just fled the room after failing to produce so much as a squeak when the string quartet's introductory bars drew to a close. When he followed her into the garden he found her throwing up into a potted fern. His lip curled in distaste as he handed her a handkerchief.

"I didn't know you suffered so badly from stage fright, my dear."

"It's nothing, just butterflies."

"Really? I hear your performances have been deteriorating for months."

"What business is that of yours?"

"Everything my not-so-niece does is my business, wouldn't you agree?"

Martezha flung the handkerchief back at him and didn't answer. He sidestepped the soiled cloth.

"It's time for one of those favours we spoke of. Urdig balks at quarantining the Vergal and I need it to happen sooner rather than later."

"I don't make policy."

"No, but you can persuade … He clings to this notion of the healers that the miasmic odours won't affect other quarters of the city. Some of them disagree and think it might be spread by less appropriate lifestyles, shall we say. The place is full of Untalents. How can one tell the clean from the unclean? What if a supplicant gets too near his precious daughter and passes it on to her? You see?"

Martezha shrugged, but agreed to try. Loric brooded as she returned to the drawing room. The Vergal! What was his pet Untalent thinking, skulking around the Vergal? Was she suicidal? It took him some time to track her down after she gave him the slip leaving the builders, but now that he had found her again—the surveillance of her healer friend paid off—he had no intention of losing her to a passing fever. His own inquiries into Padvai's past had yielded few results. But he would find a way to exploit the girl from Adram Vale yet.

∞ ∽

Interminable! That's how each day away from the Vergal felt to Saroya. The news kept getting worse: the plague spread from a small area near the port and now moved inland at an alarming rate. Tense with worry about Veshwa, Saroya feared that plague or no plague, it had been so many years since Veshwa left House Roshan that anything could have happened—she could have died years ago. Saroya refused to think about that. Veshwa was alive, and Saroya would find her.

This time, Nalini and Saroya decided to split up. Saroya wanted to knock on doors in neighbourhoods not yet afflicted by the fever, whereas Nalini wanted to explore the port. Nalini left Saroya with a list of health questions. "Might as well kill two birds with one stone, no?" They agreed to meet for lunch at a square midway between their two search areas.

"No, sorry."

"Go away!"

"There's nobody home!" This last from behind the closed door Saroya had just banged on.

Three hours of trudging up streets and alleys, and Saroya's ears rang from all the doors slammed in her face. Too many people feared the plague to open their doors to a complete stranger, and when she asked Nalini's questions, and told them she wasn't a healer, their suspicions grew. The few willing to talk to her had never heard of Veshwa. She seethed with frustration as she arrived to meet Nalini.

"Is your day going any better than mine?"

Nalini shook her head, looking footsore and weary. "I've never seen anything like it. You know that body we saw in the cul-de-sac last week?" Saroya nodded. "Well, they're dumping them everywhere now—people are dying too fast for the burial yards to keep up."

"Aren't you worried about getting sick?"

"Yes, but already, there are healers who won't set foot in the Vergal. You should see how grateful people are when they open the door and see a healer standing there. I have nothing for the fever, but I treated two burns and cleaned out three cuts this morning."

"They talk to you? I couldn't get most of them to even open the door for me." A sudden thought struck Saroya. "Do you have extra herbs in your pouch?"

Nalini eyed her suspiciously. "Yes, why?"

"They won't let me in but they'll talk to you. Maybe if I told them I was a healer's assistant, they'd talk to me too."

"But you're not a healer."

"No, and I wouldn't claim to be one either. You know I can handle cuts and bruises, and my herb knowledge isn't horrible. I'm not getting any useful answers for either you or me right now. We can use any edge we can find."

"I don't know, Saroya. The guild won't approve."

"Where's the harm? I promise not to say I'm a fully fledged healer. You haven't even finished your apprenticeship yet, and they're asking you to risk your life wandering around this infested place."

"All right, but I don't like it. You can have half of what I'm carrying, if you promise not to say you're a healer."

Saroya grinned. "You won't regret it." Another thought struck her. "Could you write me a note?"

That afternoon, herbs and parchment stating she was a healer's assistant in hand, she fared much better. The inhabitants of the Vergal seemed much more inclined to trust a healer's assistant than a stranger off the street. While she did not find anybody who knew the whereabouts of Veshwa, she diligently obtained all the information that Nalini had asked for, and made a note of the buildings where no one answered her knock. The gruelling day highlighted the monumental task ahead of her, but she was much more optimistic when, in late afternoon, she met Nalini again on the outskirts of the Vergal. Nalini looked

156 ~ KATRINA ARCHER

pale and drained.

"What's up?" Saroya asked.

"I just ran into a fellow healer and it looks like this is it for us."

"What are you talking about?"

"The plague's spreading too fast. They're going to quarantine the Vergal. The king will issue a royal decree tomorrow."

The blood fled Saroya's face. "What does it mean?"

"It means no one in or out until the decree is rescinded. Even healers who stay to help won't be allowed to travel back and forth."

"Are you staying?"

"No, I'm not a full healer and the guild wants me to finish my training first."

"How am I going to find Veshwa?"

"You'll just have to wait until this is all over."

Saroya shook her head. "By then, Veshwa could be dead." Nalini watched her as she puzzled through her options. "When does the quarantine start?"

"Tomorrow afternoon."

"Great. That gives me some time. I need you to get me more maps of the Vergal, and more healing supplies."

"I don't understand."

"I'm staying here." Saroya ignored the frightened expression on her friend's face. She had no choice. She had to stay to have any hope of finding Veshwa before the plague got her.

"You can't! You'll be stuck here for who knows how long. Where will you live?"

"I'm not sure yet, but I know who to talk to first." Saroya's mind spun. "I'll keep doing your survey for you while I'm here."

Nalini looked doubtful. Saroya grabbed her by the shoulders and stared her straight in the eyes. "I have to do this."

"I know." Nalini sniffled. "I just keep thinking, if I'd stood up for you when Eiden Callor asked me about the ring …"

"Get going—we don't have much time. Meet me tomorrow morning at the Spotted Salmon Pub. Early."

CHAPTER 10

The counter had accumulated a few more scratches since Saroya last frequented the Spotted Salmon. Balreg placed a glass of cider in front of her. "Back so soon?"

"Can we talk in private?"

He raised a greasy eyebrow, shrugged, and inclined his head towards a door in the back wall. She followed him into a combination keg storage and pantry.

"Now, what is it you don't wish my genteel clientele to hear?"

"Tell me about Veshwa."

"I don't know any Veshwa."

Saroya exhaled in frustration. "You said you could tell me about my friend."

"I said I would 'trade' for information about your friend."

"Do you have family?"

"A wife. And a son."

"I have information that can help them escape the plague."

Balreg stared at her dubiously. "All right. Spill it."

"First you tell me about Veshwa. And you agree to give me a room here for the next little while."

"What do you think this is, an inn? The upstairs barely fits my family as it is. I don't have room for you."

"You will once you hear my news."

He blew air from between pursed lips, and leaned back against a rough-hewn shelf. "Fine. A woman named Veshwa once lived near the Minor West Canal. But she's long gone from there."

"Did she die?" The knot of worry in Saroya's stomach tightened.

"I didn't hear of it if she did. Now, your turn."

Saroya ran a hand through her copper mane. He hadn't given her much to go on but a trade was a trade. "They're quarantining the Vergal tomorrow. Anybody still in the quarter after that will not be able to leave. If you have family anywhere else in the city, send your child there. I'd do it tonight, if I was you, and I'd also be discreet."

Balreg cursed. Saroya continued, "If you feel you need to stay with them, I can watch the pub for you, although I won't have time to run it."

"Why should I trust you with my pub?"

Saroya shrugged. "Trust me, don't trust me. It's your decision. I'm staying in the quarter anyway and I'd rather not have to hunt for a room."

Balreg tossed his ever-present greasy rag onto the far corner of a shelf. "Bah. Come with me—I'll show you your room." He beckoned her to follow him up a dingy stairway in the hall past the storeroom. Plague or no plague, his apartments were a step up from the hard stone of the bridge.

The next morning at dawn she sat in the empty pub room eating the skimpy breakfast Balreg's wife placed in front of her. The woman gave her a cursory tour of the kitchen before disappearing into the back alley with a small bag on her back and her son's hand clasped in hers. Balreg slid the key to the lock across the counter to Saroya before following his family, shooting parting instructions over his shoulder. "... and don't feed the cats, just leave them some water. Otherwise they get lazy and let the rats overrun the stores."

Saroya found a scrap of parchment and some ink and, hoping at least a few of the pub's clients could read and spread the word, made up a sign that she tacked onto the front door: "Closed Due to Death in Family". She was barring the door when a timid knock interrupted her. She let in a drawn-faced Nalini.

"You made it."

Nalini dropped two large bags onto the counter. "It wasn't easy. They're already setting up barricades on some of the bridges over the river. If I don't get back across the canals before word gets out I could get stuck in a riot."

"What did you bring me?"

Nalini listed the items on her fingers: two maps of the Vergal, miscellaneous herbs, ointments and compresses, several reams of parchment, spare quills and ink, a healer's belt pouch, and a basic healing text.

"Have you found a way we can pass messages and supplies back and forth?"

"Messages will be relatively easy. There's a healer staying behind—his name's Faro—and he'll have a special quarantine pass so that he can communicate with the guild. I've told him you're doing research for me and my guildmaster." Nalini passed her a small parchment with the man's details. "If he finds out you're doing anything other than 'research', I'll be in big trouble with the guild."

"He won't find out from me."

"Supplies will be harder. I'll need more time to come up with a plan. I'll let you know in a message if I figure out something else, but until then you should have enough in those bags to last you a little while."

Saroya accompanied Nalini back to the edge of the Vergal. They stopped a hundred paces from a small bridge. Saroya noted the guards and the crowd already gathered, muttering and angry at being denied exit from the Vergal.

Nalini pointed across the river. "Look, things could get bad and I may not be able to get messages to you. Do you see that square on the other side? It's within shouting distance—not private but as a last resort ... I'll come once a week at this time to see if there's anything you need."

Saroya hugged Nalini, then they parted ways. She

watched to make sure that Nalini's healer's pouch was enough to get her across the bridge and out of the Vergal then turned back to the pub. She thought she'd known loneliness before. She was wrong.

∞ ∞

Loric paced up and down while Daravela studied her fingernails.

"So you refuse to help?" he asked.

Daravela shrugged. "Someone may have tampered with Padvai's Testing, but the evidence is circumstantial, at best. I can find no proof of complicity on Urdig's part. Your wife could corroborate nothing."

"That's it then. You're washing your hands of the whole thing." Loric worried she questioned the wisdom of allying herself with him.

"I didn't say that. Are you any closer to confirming Mistress Bardan's identity?"

"My inquiries yielded nothing."

"You've been saying that for months."

"If you doubt me, feel free to end our little agreement."

"I may have a lead for you. The doyenne in Adram Vale reports that Mistress Bardan asked about a woman named Veshwa." Loric stopped pacing as Daravela continued. "If you feel matters are coming to a head, you may want to put more pressure on Urdig. I understand some Houses now lobby for greater restrictions on Untalents."

"And?"

"Urdig will oppose these efforts."

"You know this for sure?"

"His voting history and his alliances within the Great Circle make it almost certain."

"What do you propose, Eminence?"

"This plague and the Vergal quarantine offer us an opportunity. The Healer's Guild is already suspicious of the Vergal's squalor as a plague source."

"And Untalents make up a large portion of the Vergal's population."

Daravela nodded. "You see where I'm heading?"

Loric smiled. It had worked in the past, he knew. "A simple matter of a few well-placed agitators. And suddenly, Untalented equals plague carrier."

"Urdig's opposition to Untalented controls will look ill-advised—dangerous, even. Add an Untalented daughter into the mix and the Houses won't want anything to do with him. How far are you willing to go?"

"Far enough," Loric replied.

"What I'm suggesting may cause your wife's family serious problems."

"Isolte will support us." Loric would ensure she did. He could tell Daravela still had reservations about confiding in him, but after a moment she went on.

"It is my conjecture that House Roshan intentionally used Padvai's marriage to Urdig to install an Untalented queen in a position to pull strings for the family. And set up an heir for actual future rule. A hidden Untalent on the throne poses a serious threat to the Order. Roshan isn't the only House that chafes at submitting to mandatory Testing. My sources bring me whispers of a movement within the Great Circle to limit the right of the Order to Test."

Loric knew then that their bargain would hold. Daravela would never pass up the opportunity to remove such a thorn in the Order's side.

All because House Roshan had finally miscalculated after all these years.

∞ ∞

The Spotted Salmon had several advantages as a base of operations. Its central location in the Vergal allowed Saroya easy access to most neighbourhoods. Mention of Balreg or the pub opened many doors to her that would have remained closed. She fine-tuned her story: she was Balreg's niece, a failed healer the guild now allowed to conduct research on their behalf.

She began her door-to-door canvass in the area of the Minor West Canal, as per Balreg's information, asking the questions Nalini designed to find out if anything in the household poisoned the air. Saroya added her own questions regarding daily habits; while she respected Nalini, she also suspected the healers could be just as closed off to new ideas as the builders. She wasn't prepared to accept the poisoned air theory. Or the viler one she'd overheard at the fishmarket: that Untalents were the source. Suddenly it seemed more important, both for her and her fellow

Untalents, that she find the true cause. She left her questions about Veshwa to the end after her interviewees shed their suspicions.

Her first day ended with no hints of Veshwa anywhere. She covered sixty homes, making note of the doors where her knocks went unanswered. At this rate it could take her months to cover the quarter.

She fixed herself a quick meal in the pub's kitchen, checked that the sign was still posted on the barred front door, and then went up to Balreg's apartments. She unrolled the maps Nalini left her and tacked one up onto the wall. Then she dug her notes out of her pouch, marking on the map every house visited, and how many sick and healthy residents in each. She examined her questionnaires, counting the different answers for each question, with a tally of the healthy and ill in each category. She finished after midnight, her eyes burning, and no clear pattern showing itself. She crawled underneath a blanket and fell asleep, exhausted.

Late on the third day, as she neared the end of her canvass of the Minor West Canal area, Saroya wanted nothing better than to throttle the old dressmaker in front of her. Her tongue loosened in gratitude for the poultices Saroya gave her for her arthritic hands, the woman blathered on while Saroya eyed the lengthening shadows. Saroya doubted she would ever get back out the door. Benumbed, she almost forgot to ask about Veshwa as she took her leave, and was only half-listening as she prepared to make her escape.

"Veshwa, Veshwa ... I think—no that was Pashma, wait," the woman rambled.

"I should go." Saroya forced herself not to roll her eyes.

"No, just a minute. The woman who used to live four doors down ... Her name was Veshwa."

Saroya's heart skipped. *Don't get too excited*—the dressmaker's memories did not seem reliable. "Used to live?"

"She moved out a few years back."

"Where?"

"Oh, now, that I don't know, dearie."

Saroya took her leave, and then knocked on the door of Veshwa's former residence. The woman who answered was obviously feverish, and Saroya took a step back. She could give no treatment to the afflicted, and risked too much if she entered the home.

"So you have not come to save us."

Saroya shook her head helplessly. "There is no cure. I can leave you some herbs for the headaches, but there's not much more I can do. Maybe you can help me, though. I'm looking for a woman named Veshwa who used to live here."

The woman leaned against the doorframe, then shook her head. "We've been here five years. My husband owns the building. We moved in when his fishing fleet was lost in a winter storm, and we could no longer afford our other home. I remember the woman you speak of. My husband kicked her out when we needed the place ourselves. I felt sorry for her. I don't think she had any family to go to. I don't know where she went."

"No idea at all?" Saroya bit her lip.

"She may have moved to an almshouse, but I wouldn't know which one."

Saroya sighed. "Thanks, anyway," she said, depositing the promised herbs on the stoop before she left. The resignation in the woman's fevered eyes haunted her.

Back at the pub, she collated all her data and then stared glumly at the map of the Vergal. She counted at least twenty almshouses scattered across the quarter, and was sure that she'd ferret out an equal number of unmarked poorhouses on her own.

The next morning, as she prepared to leave by the back alley, a knock on the front door of the pub interrupted her. She hesitated then unbarred the door. A slender woman, hooded, stood on the stoop, clutching the hand of a young boy, barely more than a toddler.

"Please, can you help us? The healer in our neighbourhood died of the plague. I don't know what to do —Theogar won't stop coughing." Desperation shone in the woman's face.

"I'm not a healer—"

"But they said—"

"I'm only a healer's assistant. I can give you some herbs. Put them in boiling water, and let him breathe the vapours— they should help, unless he has plague. Nothing I can give you will help then."

She sent the woman away but more rapping at the door prevented Saroya from setting out on her own mission. This time, an older man held out his bandaged right hand. He'd cut it opening an oyster on the docks. Word of Saroya's presence had spread, along with her reputation for treating small wounds and ailments. With the shortage of true healers, the inhabitants of the Vergal seemed happy to settle for her paltry skills. A steady stream of patients kept her busy until lunch, when a break in the flow of people allowed her to escape.

With just the afternoon available, she only visited two almshouses and their immediate neighbourhoods. The plague rampaged through these areas. The almshouses, with their crowded, squalid conditions, acted like breeding grounds for the fever. Her knock went unanswered at the second almshouse, though she heard someone talking from deep within the building. She pushed the unlocked door ajar, and peered into the gloom.

"Hello?" Saroya's greeting echoed down the narrow hallway.

She checked the cloth tied round her face was secure then crossed the threshold. She passed two empty rooms on her way down the hall, parchments strewn on the floor. The hallway opened into another cross corridor ten paces further on. The voice she'd heard on entering resolved into a sing-song muttering. Saroya frowned. That didn't sound like an administrator. She reached the junction, where a terrible stench overwhelmed her and she gagged.

"Who's there?" A man leaped out from round the corner, a large stick in his hands held ready to strike. Saroya shrieked and stumbled backwards.

"Don't hit me!" She braced for the blow.

"Who are you? Get out!" The man thrust what Saroya could now see was only a broomstick in her face. "Go on— or fever'll getcha. Fever, reaver, leave her."

Was he mad? Saroya tried to recover her composure. She put out her hands, trying to placate him. "I'm a healer's assistant. I was hoping to see the administrator."

The man spat on the ground. "Fled, he did. Left us all here to die. Die abed, skin all red."

"Why are you still here?"

"Someone's got to burn the bodies." Saroya recoiled. He'd startled her so badly that she'd missed the sheen of fever in his eyes, but now that she looked closely, she could see the inflamed pustules spotting his skin. She cursed under her breath—why had she come in?

The man turned his back on her and scurried round the corner, spewing nonsense. Against her better judgement, she edged forward.

The foulness assailed her nostrils despite the cloth. A window in the corridor showed her the central courtyard, with a pyre piled with bloated bodies. The man, still nattering, dragged another out of the hall. Bile scorched Saroya's throat, and she ran back out to the street. She would not find Veshwa here, not alive.

After that visit, Saroya obsessed about the safety precautions Nalini had recommended: she used a different face covering every day, and boiled anything made of fabric that she'd worn outside. As soon as she returned to the pub, she threw out items that might have come into contact with a sick person, tossing them into the stove, especially the parchments on which she took all her notes. She carefully transcribed the data before throwing the originals into the fire. She washed every night, not knowing if it helped, but if Nalini was correct that some foul vapour caused the fever, she dared not risk any of it clinging to her.

At the end of the week, she went to the house Nalini had told her of and gave a report of her activities to the healer she found there. Faro looked tired and drawn, but still managed to convey his disdain for her. "A futile effort, if you ask me. We need more healers here, not note takers." Yet he took the paper from her before slamming the door in her face.

Next, Saroya set out to meet Nalini. She rounded a corner into an open square, and bumped headlong into a black-coated magistrate. Before she could think to apologize and make a quick escape, he'd grabbed her arm. Saroya gulped. Would the magistrates still be looking for a delinquent renter? As he peered at her face and dress, Saroya noticed the group of scruffy people in the cart behind him, guarded by a second magistrate.

"Talent certificate, please," the magistrate said.

"What?"

"By order of the Healer's Guild. If you can't show me proof of Talent, I'll have to take you to one of the camps."

Saroya felt as though the ground had dropped away

beneath her. She looked more closely at the people in the cart. Their hands were bound. Were they all Untalents? What new policy was this? She tried to buy time.

"I ... I never carry my certificate with me. I didn't realize I needed to."

Saroya found no sympathy in the magistrate's face. "Show me a certificate, or get in that cart."

The unfairness of it made Saroya want to kick the man in the shins. She'd been hearing vile rumours tying Untalents to the plague for days, but nothing in her own survey showed any link. The plague chose its victims indiscriminately. Saroya knew she wasn't sickening people. Those poor people in the cart weren't either. If conditions in the camps he mentioned were anything like the sick camps she'd heard whispers of, then getting into that cart was tantamount to a death sentence. No one came back from the camps. Ever.

The magistrate lost patience. He reached for the manacles at his waist.

"Wait!" Saroya cried out. She rummaged in her pouch, and pulled out Nalini's note vouching for her as a healer's assistant. "Will this do?"

The magistrate conferred with his partner as Saroya tried to look official. Finally he handed the paper back to her. "Very well. It seems you're doing important work. Better get on with it."

Saroya didn't wait around for him to change his mind. She hurried off. Relief mingled with a renewed sense of urgency. As if Untalents didn't have enough to deal with.

Now they were scapegoats for the plague. She had to find proof the healers were wrong. She had to find Veshwa. No one would listen to an Untalent trying to save her skin. But this wan't just about her anymore. With so many lives at stake, maybe the king's daughter could keep others like her from dying needlessly.

Finally, Saroya arrived at the square where she'd left Nalini. She searched the far shore of the river for her friend. She was just about to leave when she spotted a small figure emerging from an alleyway. She recognized Nalini's determined gait. At first, she couldn't place the taller man who followed her friend into the square. Saroya hurried to the water's edge, and with a sinking feeling she identified Eiden Callor.

Nalini waved to her from the opposite shore, a little sheepishly, Saroya thought. Thirty paces separated them; they didn't need to raise their voices. Saroya ignored Callor.

"I gave my report to Faro. I've been looking, but I haven't found a pattern yet."

"You look tired. Still feeling well?" Nalini asked.

"I'm not sick yet."

Eiden Callor shook his head. "Foolish girl, gallivanting about on a futile quest."

Hot indignation burned through Saroya, though she knew showing it might alienate him forever. "Gallivanting? I'm working harder now than ever. If what I discover keeps one person from falling ill then it will all be worth it."

"You know that's not what I meant."

Saroya glared at Nalini. "You told him?"

"I didn't have a choice. He came to the guild looking for you. He made me bring him here."

"Someone matching your description duped the castle fitter into giving them livery. Normally I wouldn't waste time on such a small matter but I've had enough of your games," Callor said.

Saroya addressed Callor. "I didn't have much choice either. It was either this or lose the only chance I have of proving I am who I claim to be."

"I can't believe you still insist—"

"Insist?" Saroya was shouting now. "The sheer fact I'm here, risking my life, doesn't tell you anything?" She felt her cheeks flush hot. "That stuck up, overdone, fame hungry, money-grubbing tart worms her way into the only family I might ever know and I'm supposed to take it lying down?"

Eiden Callor had the grace to look taken aback. He glanced at the bridge a hundred paces away; the noise had attracted the attention of the quarantine enforcers. Saroya took her emotions in hand with difficulty.

"You may never believe me. That's your choice. But I will leave here with proof of who I am, or knowing that proof is lost forever, or dead. There are no other options. Now, if you will excuse me, I have work to do. Nalini, I'm fine on supplies for this week but may need more next week." She wasn't sure how much Nalini had told Callor. Nalini nodded.

"I'll get you a bit more of everything."

"Surely, food is getting through," Callor said.

Nalini answered, leaving out any mention of healing supplies. "She needs parchment and the like. For her notes." This seemed to satisfy Callor.

Saroya forced a smile for her friend. "See you next week." She whirled and strode back into the Vergal, wondering if the plague would make her a liar.

∾ ∽

The plague spread at an alarming rate, leaving few houses unaffected. The burial wagons could not keep up with the bodies, and on every street Saroya walked, several lay in the gutter; nobody wanted to keep the dead in their homes. Even through her cloth shield, the stench made her gag.

Coming up a narrow passageway, Saroya heard shouting. The alley opened onto a wooden span crossing one of the canals. From where she stood in the deep shade of the buildings, she could not see over the bridge's arc. The screams got louder, punctuated by curses. Before she could decide what to do, a man stumbled over the bridge, fleeing a dozen angry pursuers. Their quarry tripped over the last step of the span, his arms windmilling before he smacked the ground. The mob closed in and pummelled him with kicks and punches. Saroya's scream caught in her throat.

"You dirty Untalent!"

Thinking the mob had spotted her, Saroya flattened herself into the shadows of a doorway.

"Making us all sick, you are."

"We won't let you spread your foul disease any more."

If the man on the ground said anything, Saroya couldn't hear. She watched in horror as he curled up in a ball, trying in vain to deflect the blows hailing down. One of his attackers, holding a length of wood, aimed a vicious crack at his victim's head. Saroya flinched. A spray of blood spattered the alley. The man on the ground convulsed once and grew still.

His assailants kicked him a few more times, then lost interest. The man with the club peered down the alley towards Saroya. She shrank against the wooden doorway, but he didn't see her. With a shout, he herded his gang back across the bridge.

Saroya waited until she was sure they were gone, then checked the huddled man on the ground. She retched. She could do nothing for him. He'd died because of someone else's irrational hatred. And for what? The plague didn't come from Untalents. It had arrived on a ship.

Shuddering, she turned back down the alley looking for an alternate route back to the pub. She clutched the healer's pouch at her waist, prepared to wave it at anyone who stared at her with the least suspicion.

The days blurred in Saroya's mind, mornings spent tending those who came to the pub for small curatives, afternoons filled trawling the Vergal for information. It was difficult to remember which days she was supposed to meet with Nalini. After dark, drunken revelers cavorted in the streets—people who felt they no longer had anything to lose by public displays of debauchery. She kept the doors to the

Spotted Salmon barred. Several times, loud pounding on the wooden slats jolted her from her work: ruffians looking for stronger drink. Rumours of rapes and worse circled through the neighbourhood and she stayed in at night to avoid trouble.

In the morning, she woke with a blinding headache. She could stomach only a few mouthfuls of almond milk from her scanty breakfast. *No, no, no. It can't be. Not the plague!*

She moaned, fear, frustration and exhaustion crashing in on her. She curled up in a corner and ignored the knocks on the door of the pub. Heat wracked her body. She rocked back and forth, unable to find a comfortable position to lie in. Her joints ached. Her lower back throbbed. Even her teeth were sore. She was going to die here and no one would be the wiser. All her searching, come to nothing. Her life, nothing as well. And Martezha, laughing from her comfortable perch in the palace. It was too much to bear.

A raging thirst roused her and she tottered to the water barrel. The cool liquid soothed her somewhat and her head cleared. While her headache receded, her anger mounted. She would not end this way. She would not. Maybe she just had a cold. No pustules had appeared yet. Filling a water skin, she set out with renewed determination. She wouldn't quit unless the fever forced her off her feet.

She had visited more than half of the almshouses and charitable establishments in the Vergal when she arrived at Abaya House. The iron gates were locked but a bell hung on the stone gateposts. She wiped perspiration from her brow before grasping the intricately knotted rope attached to the clapper and clanging for admission.

A plump woman in a brown robe hurried up the short drive, stopping well clear of the gate. Her friendly face wore an expression of firm regret.

"No visitors at this time. The plague, you know."

"I'm a healer's assistant, conducting a survey on the plague for the guild. I was hoping to speak to the administrator."

The woman pursed her lips in thought.

"Let me see what Madam Abaya says. Wait here."

Saroya leaned against the sun-warmed stone. Her gaze skimmed over a beggar stealing the boots from a plague corpse in the gutter. The sight had become all too common in the last few days. She heard crunching pebbles and turned to face the gate again.

"Madam Abaya will see you in the back garden." The woman unlocked the gate and swung it open.

They walked up the driveway, passing underneath an arch in the stone building itself before arriving at a lush green courtyard. The almshouse surrounded the courtyard on three sides. A tall wooden fence bounded the fourth. The elegant and peaceful aspect of the surroundings surprised Saroya. All the almshouses, and in fact, most of the places she'd seen in the Vergal suffered from a certain amount of decrepitude, whether from age, neglect, or poverty. Not Abaya House. The garden was well tended and the whitewash on the window frames fresh. The woman in brown gestured to a wooden bench, where another identically dressed woman sat waiting. She indicated for Saroya sit across from her. Saroya's guide disappeared into a door inset into the archway.

"You will excuse me if I do not approach," Madam Abaya said. "We have been fortunate to avoid the plague so far—the vapours do not trouble us here."

Saroya hoped the sheen of fever on her brow wasn't visible. She felt chilled now, as opposed to the scorching heat that ran through her body a few minutes ago.

"You have no fever victims here?"

"None whatsoever."

"Strange. This neighbourhood is one of the most severely afflicted."

Saroya interviewed the woman thoroughly. In the end, nothing jumped out at her. She closed her eyes to ward off a wave of dizziness. She was *not* sick!

"You seem more prosperous than other almshouses I have visited."

"Because we are not really an almshouse. We rely on the generosity of several noble Houses. We take in a few charity cases, yes, but primarily we provide sanctuary for older servants of Houses that feel they have a duty to care for loyal staff. I wish all the Houses felt that way—we might have fewer old beggars dying in the streets."

"Older House servants?" Saroya's squeaky voice sounded strange to her ears.

"Yes. Is something wrong?"

"No—no, no." She dared not hope. Her pulse pounded against her throbbing headache, and she looked around the garden for distraction. In the far corner, a girl hoisted a bucket of water out of a lichen-covered well. Saroya licked her fever-chapped lips. What she wouldn't give ... She turned back to Madam Abaya. Her voice was unsteady as she posed her question. "There, uh, there wouldn't happen to be a woman named Veshwa living here, would there?"

Madam Abaya's unreadable expression plunged Saroya into doubt. Saroya braced for yet another disappointment.

"Why do you ask?"

Saroya drew in a quick breath. How much to tell?

"She knew my mother. I ... I'm an orphan. Veshwa's my only link to my family."

"In all her time here, Veshwa has remained alone. No visits from any of the children she cared for. I expect she would be delighted to speak to you."

Another wave of dizziness swept over Saroya and it was all she could do to keep Madam Abaya's lips in focus. She must not have heard correctly. Veshwa, here? Her next words came out in a harsh whisper. "Please. You must let me see her."

"Very well. On one condition: after your visit today, you will not return until the plague passes. Not until the danger is gone."

Saroya bobbed her head in agreement. She wouldn't wish the plague even on Martezha. She'd never forgive herself if she made anybody else sick. She just had a cold, didn't she?

And Veshwa was here!

"Follow me, then."

Madam Abaya walked up an exterior stone staircase built into the walls of the almshouse. Saroya trailed after her on treads worn by years of passing feet. She gripped the banister with a shaky hand, overtaken by nervousness. They ignored the first landing, entering the almshouse on the third floor, where Madam Abaya stopped in front of a plain oak door. She motioned for Saroya to wait as she entered the room. When she returned, she looked concerned.

"Veshwa will see you now. Please do not overtire her. Can you find your way out afterwards?" Saroya nodded. "Then go on in. Good luck."

Saroya took a deep breath and pushed open the door. The room that greeted her was not at all what she expected after the dark warren-like rooms of the other almshouses she had visited. Bright sunlight streamed in through large windows. A multitude of coloured cushions and tapestries enlivened spartan furniture. At first, she thought the room empty, but her confusion subsided when she spotted the elderly woman lying propped up in the bed. The woman reached out a frail, liver-spotted hand and patted the seat beside the bed.

"Come, sit. We can stare out at the garden together."

"I'm not feeling very well. I think it's just a cold, but I don't want to make you sick."

Veshwa snorted. "At my age, that's the least of my worries."

Saroya crossed the room and sat down in the chair.

Veshwa tried to grip her hand but Saroya eluded the touch—she could at least avoid sickening Veshwa.

"Don't you want to know my name?" Saroya asked.

"My dear, I would have known your face anywhere. That hair, those lips …"

Tears glistened in Veshwa's eyes. Despite Veshwa's age, what if the uncertainty that had worried Saroya since speaking to Kimila was true? That Veshwa might be her mother, not Padvai. What if Veshwa left Roshan service in disgrace because she'd borne a child, not because she hid Roshan secrets?

"They are the same as your mother's, and so, you can only be Saroya."

A single, harsh sob escaped Saroya. "So it's true, then, you knew my mother?"

Veshwa laughed. "Knew her? I probably knew her better than she knew herself." Veshwa picked up a silver comb, her hand trembling arthritically. "I used to comb the knots in her hair with this. I was her nursemaid, and then her personal lady-in-waiting until she married Urdig."

"That's what Kimila told me."

"Kimila! Still kicking around House Roshan, is she?" Veshwa smiled, then turned serious. "Now, child, why are you here? It's dangerous for someone of your stature to be out alone in the Vergal these days. Although I commend you on your choice of disguise. Very effective."

Puzzled, Saroya blurted, "My stature?"

"The royal princess, breaking plague quarantine. Why, if anybody found out …"

"You don't understand. I'm not the royal princess."

Veshwa stared at her, aghast. "But I heard the news months ago—you'd been found! I was so happy to discover you weren't an Untalent after all. Who is the woman in the castle?"

"Her name is Martezha."

"I thought it must be a name they gave you in Adram Vale. How does she come to be there in your place?" Veshwa gripped the quilted coverlet spread across her legs, wringing and worrying at the fabric.

"The ring with the blue stone. She stole it. Nobody believes me." Saroya wasn't interested in rehashing the theft. "I am Untalented. Is that why my mother left me at the Cloister?"

"I left you there, but yes, that is the reason."

"Was it … was it hard for her, at least?" Saroya could barely get the words out. The answer might sear her heart.

"Oh, child. It was the hardest thing she ever did. Harder even than leaving her first love to marry Urdig."

"But she couldn't have known I was Untalented when I was born."

"She couldn't risk it. House Roshan kept it quiet—but Padvai herself was an Untalent. Something in the family line produces Untalents—more often than normal.

"So she knew?"

"No. She planned to hide any child she bore until its

Talent showed itself. The Adepts at the Cloister were to notify me as soon as that occurred."

"Why you?"

Veshwa picked the comb out from a fold of the quilt, and turned it over in her hands.

"I had raised her and knew her secret. When she conceived, she arranged to spend time in the countryside and bore her child, you, Saroya, at her father's estate in Tarash. Then I brought you to the Cloister in Adram Vale, pretending you were mine and that I could not keep you—I was too poor."

"So if I was Talented I'd be acknowledged?"

"I assume so."

Saroya absorbed this in silence for a moment.

"Did the king know my mother was Untalented?"

Veshwa's hand holding the comb stilled. "I'm not sure. He might have suspected. But he loved Padvai. Isolte never forgave Padvai for that."

"Her sister?"

"Your aunt. Isolte expected to make the better marriage, but their father insisted that Padvai go to Urdig. Even though she loved another. Airic was adamant. Padvai to Urdig, and Isolte to Loric."

Fascinated, Saroya drank in every word. To have a family, which had a history, painful as it was—even looking in from the outside, was more than Saroya had ever hoped. Her family, her people. They had rejected her, but they couldn't keep her from her roots.

Veshwa read her expression.

"Your mother loved you. To her, it didn't matter whether you were Talented or not. But she had a duty to her husband, and the throne."

"Then this is it? I go through life letting Martezha take my place? Letting my father believe a lie? And what about me, then? What happens to me?" Duty to the throne. Didn't the throne have a duty to all its subjects? Untalents included? Certainly a girl like Martezha wouldn't see it that way. Saroya thought of all she could do for people like her if she was in Martezha's place instead.

Veshwa patted her hand. "That, I cannot answer." She pointed at a small wooden box sitting on top of a table in the corner. "Fetch that for me, please."

Saroya retrieved the box and set it on the bed next to Veshwa. The old woman unlatched a small clasp and rummaged inside.

"Here. Go to House Roshan and show this to Dhilain. It will tell him who you are." Veshwa dropped a delicate loop of gold inset with amethysts in Saroya's palm.

"Dhilain?"

"Padvai's brother—now the head of Roshan."

The metal loop looked like a ring, but twisted in odd places like no ring Saroya had ever seen. "What is it?"

"One piece of a ring that fits together like a puzzle. Ashra gave it to her first daughter, and Padvai split it into pieces at your birth. She told me to give it to you if you ever presented yourself."

"Dhilain has the other piece?" Saroya turned the ring over and over in her hands. Such a small thing to hinge so much of her life upon.

"I don't know. He knows the ring—it's a family heirloom."

"Why would he acknowledge an Untalent?"

"He might not. But one thing I learned in my years serving Roshan … We all grow up being told what a stigma it is. But House Roshan embraced it, like a badge of honour."

"Yet they hid their Untalents from the world." *Hid me.*

"True, but behind their own walls, an Untalented child was treated just as any other. Maybe better. Padvai was Airic's favourite."

"Then why hide me in Adram Vale, and not closer to the House?" But she knew the answer, though it pained her to admit it. House Roshan was not the same as the king's House. An Untalent's welcome would be very different there.

"Isolte made Padvai wary. Isolte doesn't share the family tolerance for Untalents."

Veshwa stifled a yawn.

"I've tired you!"

"No, child, I just can't keep awake for as long as I used to. Napping keeps me busy these days."

Saroya wracked her mind for any other questions. "You know I won't be able to visit you again."

"Yes. But I suspect I'll still be here for you to talk to once the whole thing has blown over."

"You don't seem worried."

"Child, at my age, there isn't much to worry over anymore. What will come, will come. I stopped fighting long ago. At least Padvai's gratitude keeps me in a clean place, and well fed."

Saroya wanted to hug Veshwa. She settled for blowing her a kiss from the door.

"Good luck, child. I hope Dhilain treats you well."

Saroya walked down the hall, but as she reached the head of the stairs, the dizziness overtook her again. This time, instead of passing, it worsened and her vision narrowed to a small point of light. She put out a hand to find the banister but it eluded her. The last thing she heard before she fainted was Madam Abaya's dismayed shout from the end of the hall.

CHAPTER 11

Eiden Callor joined Urdig on the king's private balcony.
Urdig gazed south at the columns of smoke rising from the
Vergal. Funeral pyres. Callor hoped one particularly thick
billowing cloud rising from the port area wasn't the
granaries. The city could ill afford losing its grain stocks.

"So the quarantine holds," Urdig said.

"For now. My new worry is the rumours." Callor's fingers
drummed against the balustrade.

"Plague and quarantine, hearsay and quacks. They go
hand in hand. People will latch onto anything if it gives them
hope."

"These are more persistent than the usual. And not about
hope. Even though the first plague ship arrived from Kurtya,
some claim the fever is the fault of the Untalents."

"What, they're dirty and useless so they must have
spawned the plague?"

Callor frowned. "Something like that."

Urdig's eyes narrowed, and he leaned forward. "Do you agree with this 'talk'?"

"I believe in the law of the realm."

"That's not what I asked."

Callor held himself very still. "No."

"Padvai had a soft spot for you. I think she saw you as the son she never had. It was on Dhilain's recommendation that I took you on, despite your youth. I had my doubts, but you fought well on the last border campaign. Do you remember?"

"Very well, My Lord."

"Then don't feed me any hogwash."

"I don't like it. It feels like simple bigotry to me."

"Good." Urdig handed Callor a leather-bound book.

"What's this?"

"A history of the Great Plague. Not one you'll find in any other library. I've been hearing rumours as well."

Callor fingered the pages of the book.

"The guilds and the Adepts incite rallies against Untalents—using the plague as an excuse. It's no longer enough to simply purge them from the guild ranks, apparently. The Healer's Guild rounds them all up—expelling them from the city. They say it's for the good of the plague carriers. There's not much I can do—the Houses support the effort."

"And this book?"

"An interesting read. Three hundred years ago, the Order of Adepts and the guilds wielded far less influence. They used the Great Plague as an excuse to secure more power. All on the backs of the Untalented. I wonder if they perpetrated a great injustice in the name of public safety. If history now repeats itself."

Callor caught his breath. He had heard vague whisperings that such a book existed, but to hold it in his hands … And that Urdig should be the one to give him such a seditious item … Agreeing with the views in this book was tantamount to treason. Callor marvelled at his liege's trust. What had Padvai told him?

A parchment fluttered out of the book. Callor picked it up then realized what it was. Queen Padvai's certificate of Talent.

"This is yours," Callor said as he passed it back to Urdig.

Urdig shrugged. "It's worthless. A forgery."

Urdig's acknowledgement shocked Callor. He paused, a thousand questions in his head, but only asked one. "Why did you marry her?"

"At the time of our wedding, I had no reason to doubt its authenticity."

Callor thought of his own certificate, sitting forgotten in a leather parchment holder in his desk. As guard captain, he'd had no need to show it in years. He hated himself for what he had to say next. "But later, if she told you—surely the fraud was reason enough to put her aside?"

"Callor, should you ever fall in love, you'd know I could do no such thing." Urdig kept his gaze trained on the Vergal. "Talented or Untalented—all the subjects of Veyle are my responsibility. Padvai taught me that. But if it comes down to a confrontation in the Great Circle of Houses, I'm no longer certain I'd have the support of the majority. Someone has been lobbying hard. My sources tell me Tikla. I have my doubts—he's never been a creative thinker."

"I fear Lord Dorn is up to no good," Callor said.

"I'm not a fool, Callor. I know he wants the throne at any cost."

"Then why provide you with the key to identifying your heir? Admit it—the coincidence is striking. Isolte points out these students and an heir pops out of the woodwork?"

"Any advantage Loric might have gained is long gone."

Eiden Callor's thoughts turned to a red-headed girl in the Vergal. He wondered again if he should tell Urdig about her then shook his head. "I'm not so sure."

∞ ∞

Saroya burned. Burned with fever, with the ache of muscle attempting to escape the parched skin that trapped it. In Saroya's fevered delirium, Martezha laughed, throwing scalding tea in Saroya's face over and over again. She slapped away a hand, mistaking the cooling cloth it placed on her forehead for another of Martezha's tricks. A ring of anonymous faces stared down, pointing, whispering. Were they mocking her? Were they real?

"King's bane ... your fault ... tainted ..." Accusing voices whispered above her head.

Saroya shivered. Clammy fabric twisted and ensnared her

limbs. She thrashed and flailed, but could not escape. Now she yearned for warmth, the kind of warmth her bones had not known for endless frigid days. She drowned in icy waters yet nobody heard her screams.

"... might all get sick ... giving up ... won't survive the night ..."

The meaningless snatches of conversation receded. Saroya sank beneath waves of freezing cold.

∾ ∽

"I'll look like a fool."

"Come now, Martezha, you're being unreasonable." Martezha's petulance irked Loric.

"First you made me push for the quarantine, now you want me to get it lifted. He won't listen to me. The Houses already complain he hasn't done enough."

"The Houses are the least of Urdig's worries. The plague has jumped the quarantine boundary. If he doesn't lift the quarantine so healthy people can flee the city, he'll be blamed for more deaths than any king since Pallen of Roshan took the fall for the Great Plague."

"I'm not stupid—nor is he. Let people leave and spread it outside U'Veyle? Too risky."

"That was when the quarantine was working. You whisper your doubts in his ear, I lobby for the same with the Great Circle of Houses: he'll come around."

"But why? So more people can die?"

"Isolate yourself in the castle and it will not matter to

you, my dear."

Loric strode back to the stable yard, cursing the need for this ruse. What had possessed that ninny of an Untalent to stay behind in the Vergal during a dangerous quarantine? At first when she disappeared he'd presumed she'd fled the city, until his man following her healer friend spotted them having words across the quarantine boundary. Did she believe herself immune to the fevers? He was not going to let his best potential hold over Urdig die. When he mentioned the name Daravela had given him to Isolte, she'd remembered an old House servant. Isolte thought nothing of the woman's disappearance from her brother's household at the time. The spies Loric ordered to ferret out Veshwa's location had missed their last information drop. Loric presumed the fevers took them, or they'd abandoned their mission. Money only went so far towards overcoming a person's better judgement. It never ceased to amaze him just how far it would go, though.

∽ ∾

Saroya woke to find a brown-clad woman above her squeezing water from a cloth. Saroya licked at the drops as they hit her cracked lips. She felt weak and dizzy, but lucid.

"Where am I?"

"In a bed at Abaya House. A moment—I will fetch Madam Abaya."

Saroya turned her head on the pillow and gazed out the window as she waited for Madam Abaya to appear. A light rain fell outside, glistening the leaves of the adjacent willow tree. She could see over the canal at the back of the building into drab courtyards. Forgotten laundry hung limply in the rain, a stark contrast to the lushness of the Abaya House gardens. Saroya wondered if the clothing's owners still lived.

Madam Abaya bustled in. She pressed a hand to Saroya's forehead.

"Well, the fever is gone, at least."

"How long have I been here?"

"Three days too long. Do you realize how much damage you've likely done?"

"It mustn't have been the plague if I'm still here talking to you." Saroya tried to sit up but in her weakened state, failed.

"Oh, it was definitely the plague: fever, pustules, and everything."

"That's impossible. I interviewed hundreds of people in the Vergal and never met a single one who recovered."

Disregarding Saroya's modesty, Madam Abaya flipped back the sheet covering Saroya. Saroya could not deny the evidence of the pustule scars all over her skin. She shuddered.

"I don't understand."

"Neither do I. Although I suspect whatever is protecting this house and its occupants did you a very large favour."

Saroya blinked at her. Madam Abaya continued. "You may stay here until you regain your strength. Then I want you gone. Knowingly or not, you brought the sickness into this house."

Saroya nodded her acquiescence. Fair was fair.

Two days later she paused at a tall window to admire the garden one last time before re-entering the squalor of the Vergal. She'd been puzzling about the continued health of the Abaya House occupants. She stared down at the lush greenness, thinking hard. A kitchen maid crossed the garden, bucket in hand. A question struck Saroya, and she trotted back to Madam Abaya's office, where the administrator looked up at her in irritation.

"Do you all drink from that well in the garden?"

"That's a strange question."

"Not really. I've seen enough kitchens to know—nobody cooks with well water in this city. Fountain water only. Yet your cook draws from the well." Saroya crossed her arms. "So, do you all drink it too?"

Madam Abaya nodded. "The almshouse is badly located. There's no fountain nearby large enough to support all the people here. We asked for an extension to the aqueduct but it keeps getting delayed. We decided to risk it. There's never been a problem."

Saroya gazed back out the window at the well. "Keep drinking from it."

∞ ∞

The next morning, back at the Spotted Salmon, Saroya awoke feeling refreshed for the first time in days. Not only had she found Veshwa, but a pattern had emerged from the data she collected for Nalini, one that exonerated Untalents. She suspected that the Abaya House well water offered some protection from, if not a cure for, the plague as well. She could think of no other reasonable explanation for her recovery. The air at Abaya House was the same air everyone else in the Vergal breathed, the food similar. While there, she only ingested the water her caregivers forced into her during her fever.

Now she needed a way out of the Vergal. The wait until her meeting with Nalini loomed before her. She debated risking another foray into the Vergal; would she get sick again if she talked to other victims of the fever?

She tidied up her breakfast dishes, but a banging on the door interrupted her. She almost ignored it then decided that if someone needed help, she should provide it one last time. She opened the door to find a gravid woman clutching the hand of a young boy who could not be more than six years old. Before Saroya could ask what the matter was, the woman bent over in pain, clutched her belly, and moaned.

"Healer, the baby—it's coming. The midwife is dead. I have nowhere else to go."

Saroya debated what to do. She neglected to disabuse the woman as to her title. She'd watched Durin foal a mare at the stables in Adram Vale, but beyond that, she'd never participated in a birth.

"Please—please help me." The woman swayed as another contraction tightened its grip.

How hard can it be? Saroya glanced at the boy. *She's already done it once, and second children are usually easier, aren't they?* But she'd promised Nalini she wouldn't. She should call Healer Faro.

The woman grabbed Saroya's wrist and groaned. There was no time to get Faro. If she'd figured out the plague she could certainly do this.

Now, in the middle of the night, Saroya regretted her decision to let the woman in. The labour had gone from regular prolonged but manageable contractions that the woman was able to work through, to a bloody horror. The woman's screams of pain had faded to exhausted moans, and Saroya was at her wits' end. Nothing she knew about healing or foaling prepared her for this. Saroya could see the woman's strength ebbing away, but still, the baby would not come.

"Is … is it always like this?" the woman asked.

"Surely your first wasn't so difficult?" Saroya asked.

The woman's eyes searched out the boy, who cowered in the corner, frightened by her cries and the blood.

"That's my sister's son. I took him in when the fever took her."

Another terrible spasm wracked her body and a new look crept into her eyes; Saroya saw in it the woman's realization that she might not live. A tiny arm appeared from between her legs and Saroya knew she had little time left. The baby was in the wrong position and she had no idea what to do. She turned to the boy and pulled him up by the arm.

"Do you know this place?" She rattled off the location

of Faro's rooming house. The boy nodded. "Then go. Wake up the healer there and bring him. Hurry." The boy ran off. Saroya watched his spindly legs disappear into the night.

"You're not a healer?" Despair tinged the exhaustion in the woman's voice.

Saroya bit her lip. "I'm helping the healers gather information about the plague."

"I thought … I'm dying now, and you aren't even a real healer …" She closed her eyes and for an instant Saroya really thought she was dead. When she opened them again the accusation in her eyes pierced Saroya's core. The woman said nothing, but Saroya understood. It was her fault. This woman and her baby might die, all because of Saroya's ignorance and misplaced pride. Nalini was right: Saroya was a danger to others.

Please let her live. I'll never lie about what I can do again, if she just lives. Saroya reached for a damp cloth and wiped the perspiration from the woman's brow.

"You're not going to die. Just hold on a little bit longer."

The next few minutes stretched and stretched, the longest of Saroya's life. As the woman struggled to bring a new soul into the world, Saroya for the first time felt deserving of the contempt flung at her on a daily basis.

The front door of the pub swung open with a bang, and Healer Faro stood limned by moonlight in the doorway. He strode across the room and shouldered Saroya aside.

He examined the woman with efficient hands and murmured reassurances. In curt, terse tones, he demanded hot cloths from Saroya while he asked the mother to turn over so she was on her hands and knees. Saroya thought the woman too exhausted to comply but she heaved herself over with a strength born of desperation. "Oblique, blast it …" Without delay, Faro inserted his hand between the woman's legs. Saroya watched in horrified fascination as he manipulated the baby until its arm disappeared back inside the mother. Operating by feel alone, he did something Saroya could not see. Letting out a satisfied noise, he removed his hand. A wrinkled and bloody leg popped into view. "Breech. Not ideal, but much better. Now, I know you are tired, but you must push."

The woman shook her head, beyond her limits. Yet she gritted her teeth, and bore down again. Saroya couldn't believe it when the baby slid out, covered in slick, glistening blood. She was even more surprised when it let out a weak cry—she had been sure it wouldn't survive. A faint smile crossed the woman's lips as she held her child to her breast. The little boy ran up to her and nestled under her shoulder. The healer asked the woman a question Saroya couldn't hear, and the mother pointed at Saroya.

Healer Faro made the woman comfortable then turned to Saroya. "Gather your things. You will come with me in the morning to answer to the Healer's Guild. You knew I was close by—I've never seen such reckless disregard for a person's well-being." Saroya fled up the stairs, unable to face the condemnation in his eyes.

She stripped out of her bloody tunic, discarding it on the

floor. Then she located a leather string and threaded it through the ring Veshwa had given her, before tying it around her neck and slipping it under the folds of the clean tunic she donned. She gathered her remaining notes and folded them into her spare pouch. She hesitated before deciding not to jot down her conclusions, and hid the pouch under a loose floorboard. The maps she left for Balreg. Then she sat down on the bed to contemplate her failures and await her fate. The thought of escaping by the back door and losing herself in the warren of the Vergal occurred to her, but in the end, she couldn't hide from herself.

Faro tromped up the stairs to fetch her at dawn. He had located the woman's family and ensured she had a place to rest and recuperate. After securing the pub, Saroya followed him meekly down the road. They arrived at his rooming house, where he thrust her into an empty cupboard and barred the door, saying nothing.

Hours later, Saroya heard him approach again, accompanied by at least one other person. The door to the cupboard creaked open and Saroya blinked in the sudden brightness. Someone grabbed her by the arm and pulled her into the room.

"This guardsman will take you to the guildhall, where you will be put on trial for impersonating a healer."

"What about the quarantine?"

She thought he wouldn't deign to answer. But he said, "The plague has spread outside the Vergal into the rest of U'Veyle. The guild and the king agree that quarantining the

Vergal is now pointless. So we are all free to travel within the city limits. However much that means anymore." As the guard led her away to face the guild, Saroya tried to warn Faro—his cheeks now flushed and a thin film of perspiration beading his forehead.

"Faro, the fever—if it takes you, I can help you." She could never make up for what she'd done to the woman but no one else would die of plague if she could help it.

The guard yanked her arm, but she resisted. Faro's lip curled. "You are not a healer. You can't help me, or anyone."

"But I know where you can find a cure!"

"Feeble—did you think to sway me with such an outrageous lie? Take her away."

The guard pushed her into the passage and led her down the stairs. Would the healer, once aware of his own death sentence, change his mind?

∞ ∽

"Guilty."

Saroya stared around the room, but did not find a single friendly face. Hostile healers filled the ranks of benches. She turned back to face the master healer.

"For the crime of impersonating a healer, and endangering the life of a patient, the defendant is to be placed in the prison camp for criminal Untalents."

Saroya's heart sank. The ruling was tantamount to a death sentence. Plague had already killed half the population of the newly cobbled-together prison camp outside the city. She started to shake. She watched helplessly as a senior Adept approached the master healer. The Adept handed him a note. The master healer frowned.

"It seems I have been overruled. The defendant is thus given into indenture. Bond has already been sold."

The assembled healers rose as one and bowed to the master healer, who bowed back and exited the room without a backward glance. A guard led Saroya out a side door as the rest of the healers filed out.

Back in her cell, Saroya stared at the wall, her mind vacant. A trickle of water oozed down the canal-side wall where mortar was missing from the stonemasonry. Indenture. Sold as property. Maybe she had known it would come to this. Still, better life as a slave than the death camps. Right?

A distant part of her registered the scrape of the bar across the door as somebody hauled at it, and the splash of a foot sloshing through one of the puddles on the floor, but she did not rouse from her stupor until she sensed a presence next to her. Nalini sat on the decrepit stool next to her pallet.

"Did the baby live?" Saroya braced herself.

"It wasn't a sure thing for a long while but everyone's all right."

"I thought I could handle it. I promise it will never happen again. I didn't get it before. Now I do."

Nalini bit her lip. "Why should I believe you'll stick to this promise any more than the last one? I can't stay long.

Mother's got a fever and if I don't do something to help I'll go crazy."

"Listen—I think I found something that cures the plague."

Nalini shook her head. "After all this—all the lies you told—I can't believe you'd stoop to this."

"I'm not lying!" But why should Nalini believe her? She'd lied too often. To Nalini, to herself. How could she expect anyone to believe her now? Now when she most needed them to, with so many lives at stake.

"A plague cure. You expect me to believe you just stumbled upon it? Something healers have been looking for ever since the last Great Plague?" Nalini stormed to the door.

She had to try to make Nalini see. See beyond her lies to the truth. "Look, believe me or not, but for the sake of your mother, if you go to Aba—"

"I don't want to hear it."

Saroya lifted her tunic to show Nalini her pustule scars but Nalini was already in the hall. Saroya called out. "If my new master lets me have paper, I'll write once I'm settled."

"I'd rather you not."

∞ ∾

The creak of hinges woke Saroya from a restless nap. A man she did not recognize beckoned her out.

"Where are we going?"

"Shut yer yap and follow me."

He led her up the stone stairs of the guild cellar and out into a courtyard at the rear of the building. Saroya blinked; even the watery grey light of this drizzly day was more than the lamplight she'd seen during her days awaiting trial. A cart driver sat waiting at the reins of a delivery wagon. The guard shoved her into the bed of the wagon. He clambered in after her and lashed her hands to a post. The driver slapped the reins on his mule's hindquarters and the cart lurched off. She braced herself against a heavy barrel, looking for a dry spot wedged in among the goods within the reach of the post.

They exited the gates of the Healer's Guild enclave, right into the middle of an angry mob. Guards at the gate stood elbow to elbow, swords drawn. Hurled stones bounced off the guards' shields. One rock grazed Saroya and she ducked behind the barrel. She heard desperate shouts and pleas for healing herbs and fever remedies.

"Why is the guild doing nothing? We're dying out here … Let's see how fast a cure comes when you all get sick."

The cart driver urged the mule into a trot. The mob parted grudgingly to make way, until one man raised his voice.

"Is that an Untalent ye've got there? Goin' to the pens, is she?"

The cart driver shook his head. "Those aren't me orders."

The attention of the crowd shifted to the cart.

"Why's she tied up?

Another voice shouted, "So's she can't spread the plague … So's she can't wander round givin' it t'all of us."

"Why're the healers gettin' rid of her then?"

"So's she can't spread the fever to them."

"She'll just give it to us … Get her!"

The cart driver whipped his mule. A rock hit the barrel Saroya leaned against and she shrank down. The driver cursed. "You'll get me killed, girl." Saroya stared wide-eyed at him. Did he think she was egging them on?

CHAPTER 12

More missiles pelted the cart. Saroya kicked at hands that reached for her over the edge of the cart. The driver snapped his whip at two men blocking the cart. The path ahead cleared as the mob closed in from three sides. The mule broke into a lumbering canter and suddenly they were free of the shouted invective and hail of projectiles.

Saroya shook with relief when they crossed the Healer's Canal and cleared the confrontation. Could they really hate her that much? So much that they'd kill her just because she was Untalented? She wasn't making people sick. She knew it. She could heal them if only she could tell the right person about the well. She thought Nalini was that person but she'd been wrong.

And what about all the Untalents being subjected to the same treatment or worse? If she could give the city a cure to the plague, would all their lives get better as a result? Would people stop comparing the Untalented to roaches? Give them the benefit of the doubt? Surely the Talented would have to admit the usefulness of even Untalents then.

The cart bumped across U'Veyle. The driver avoided the central Market Square, then turned southeast, crossing a single canal before veering left onto the main thoroughfare to the Grand Plaza. For a moment, she wondered if he was taking her to the castle, but he angled left in the plaza, scattering pigeons and gulls—the driver headed for the Manor District. The cart turned down the northernmost spur off Manor Circle, then onto an unfamiliar boulevard, and stopped in front of an imposing iron gate. By this time, Saroya was soaked from the rain, but she could do nothing about her bedraggled appearance. The mule's hooves echoed on the stone drive as they approached the house. Saroya caught a glimpse of an even more imposing gate to one side of the property, and understood that however grand the entrance they just passed through, it was still the back door. She swallowed.

The house they approached succeeded in looking both opulent and threatening at the same time. The dark grey stone was carved with fantastic creatures. Tall thin windows squinted at the lawns. The perfectly groomed grounds sloping down to the canal on the south side of the property discouraged casual walks.

The cart stopped with a jerk in front of a heavy oak door. A thin woman with a sour face waited for them on the steps. She waved impatiently for the driver to untie Saroya and let her down then paid him with a few coins. He left in haste.

"Hurry up, there's no dawdling around here." The woman's nasal voice grated on Saroya's ears. She followed her into the manor and stood dripping on the slate floor, not sure where to go now.

"What did I just tell you about dawdling?"

Saroya spotted the woman on a narrow set of stairs and hurried after her. She soon found herself in a tiny attic room, which hadn't been swept for cobwebs in years. The woman thrust a bundle of dry clothes into Saroya's hands and ordered her to get changed.

"When you're done, come back down to the kitchen and clean the oven."

The woman spun on her heels to leave. Saroya hesitated only slightly before asking, "Excuse me, but—what is your name and where am I?"

"You need no other name for me but 'Mistress'. Your bond was purchased by House Dorn and this is the family seat." She marched out of the room.

House Dorn! Saroya's mind raced. Hadn't her mother's sister married into House Dorn? She couldn't decide if this news was a stroke of good luck or yet another setback. On the one hand, Isolte was family. On the other, Veshwa warned her about Isolte's jealousy of Padvai—would she feel the same about Saroya? Saroya resolved to keep to herself for a while. She'd gain nothing by approaching a potential ally in the wrong manner. That was one thing she'd learned from her failures with Nalini.

She shrugged a clean tunic over her head. For years, Saroya admired the Adepts' simple silvery grey robes, imagining that one day she might wear one herself, perhaps with a sash of green for growing, or blue for healing, or even the brown of the Builder's Guild. She hadn't dared to hope that one day her own robe might be embroidered with the trim of a master Adept, much less the subtle golden gilt of a doyenne, but she'd never pictured herself without that robe or the crest of a guild emblazoned on her tunic. Much less wearing the shameful, dark slate grey clothes of the indentured.

Back in the kitchen Saroya discovered the practical reasons for drab grey instead of livery in the House colours. Any dirty job, Mistress gave to her. No one spoke a word of welcome. After scouring the oven and disposing of the ashes in the bins where they would be kept for soap-making days, Saroya took out the chamber pots. The smell clung to her fingers; one of the houseguests had been ill in the night, splattering foulness all over his bowl. Mistress scowled on inspecting the floor Saroya scrubbed next. The woman clouted Saroya's ear so hard Saroya's vision blurred. "You missed a spot." As soon as Saroya finished one job, she scurried off to the next. Her stomach growling, she finally approached Cook. "Please, is there anything to eat, maybe just a little bread?"

"I'm not here to aid you in shirking your duties. Off with you, now. I'll give you a good lashing next time."

Her evening meal consisted of the leavings of a botched

stew and a hard slice of bread. Mistress added Saroya's food, lodging and clothing costs to the price of her bond. House Dorn was not in the habit of letting indentured servants take advantage of the House hospitality. After deducting these costs from her daily wage, only a pittance remained to put against buying back her bond. At the current rate, Saroya might obtain her freedom in ten years or so.

On the evening of her second day, she crouched on her hands and knees cleaning the grate of the library fireplace. She heard the scuff of a shoe against the carpet, and her heart sank. The man padding into the room must be Lord Dorn. She was supposed to deal with the grate hours ago, but a crisis of spilled oil in the kitchens held her up. She did her best to appear unobtrusive as she laid fresh logs for the fire. Lord Dorn looked up from the letter he was reading as the last log slipped from her hands and thudded to the floor.

"I expect quiet in my library."

Saroya glanced up to see him casting her a disapproving look. She scrambled upright and bowed low. "My apologies, Lord Dorn."

"See that it does not happen again."

"Yes, My Lord." She gathered up her cleaning gear, preparing to flee the room.

"Wait … You're the new girl, are you not?"

Saroya bowed again.

"Your bond was quite the bargain."

Saroya kept her eyes on the carpet. "My Lord?"

"Most of your ilk who aren't plague-ridden have little

experience at housework. Fallen guild types, and the like. Their pride gets in the way." She heard a rustle as he tossed the letter onto a table. "Oh, rise. I've had enough bowing and scraping for one day."

She looked up at him warily. Was she expected to leave now? An appropriate answer to his last statement evaded her. He sauntered up to her. His slate-coloured eyes pierced hers.

"And you, girl ... Are you filled with pride? Was it your downfall? Or is the rest of the world to blame for all your problems?"

Whatever she said would just get her into more trouble. She dipped a curtsy and tried to leave, but he put out a hand to stop her. She froze as his fingers reached for the lanyard about her neck.

"What's this?" he whispered. She glanced down at the twisted ring.

"It's ... a family treasure." When his fingers tightened, she thought he might rip it from her throat. "Please don't take it away—it's all I have of my mother's."

"Your mother." He let go of the lanyard and backed up a pace, appraising her. "It's an unusual piece of jewelry—it doesn't look like a real ring."

So far, Saroya had not found this man likeable at all, nor did she trust him. His stare was too calculating. Yet, she needed an ally if she wanted to get the well water from Abaya House into the hands of the sick. The thought of endless indenture, knowing that Martezha stood in the position that was rightfully hers, galled her. "It's one piece of a puzzle ring."

It was subtle, but she thought his smirk now seemed satisfied. "Would it interest you to know that I have seen another, similar ring?"

Saroya held her breath. She stood on dangerous ground, here. Why was he so interested in the ring? He was her uncle, yet Veshwa warned her that currents of ambition ran through this family that she'd do well to navigate with care. Maybe he thought she'd stolen it.

"Is My Lord accusing me of something?"

He laughed, and she relaxed slightly. "No. The design of that ring is distinctive. I have never seen another like it, until now. The place I used to see it was about the neck of Queen Padvai." He believed her! But why did she feel like a mouse being hunted by a hawk? "You don't seem surprised."

"Neither do you." Her answer spilled out before she remembered she was supposed to be a meek and cowed servant. This time, his laugh rang with true mirth.

"Whatever lack of Talent you suffer from does not apply to reading people, apparently. No—I am not surprised. I've known for some time that the woman Urdig calls his daughter is an imposter. Until now, I've had no proof pointing to the true heir. I still don't, really—not until we can compare your ring with Padvai's."

He sat down on a cushioned settee and motioned that she do so as well. She lowered herself to the edge of a hard chair.

"It's no coincidence I'm here," she observed.

"Not really. I have been following the lives of all the students from Adram Vale. Discreetly. Buying your bond let me … get to know you." He leaned forward. "You don't trust me."

"I—if you've been so suspicious, why didn't you say anything to the king?"

"My dear, Martezha has a solid claim—one does not cast aspersions lightly. I am many things, but I am not a fool."

"But the king is your brother-in-law."

"Why have you not come forward before now?"

Her hand moved to the ring at her throat. "I tried, but they called me a liar. I had no proof."

"You see?"

She nodded.

Loric reached out. "If you give me the ring—"

Saroya shook her head. "I lost my only proof once. You can't have it."

Loric's fingers curled into claws but he drew back. "Very well. I will ask Isolte to find out what happened to Padvai's ring upon her death. If it is in Urdig's possession, I will obtain you a royal audience."

Saroya wanted to fall to her knees in gratitude. She could not fathom how her fortunes had turned around so quickly. With a royal audience she could tell the king himself about the well. Loric stood up.

"Until we can confirm a match, I expect you to tell no one of this. You will act exactly as the servant you are. It would not do to spread premature rumours. Understood?"

She nodded.

"Very well. Return to your duties."

She backed out of the room, bobbing several grateful bows. Then she fled to the kitchen. She longed for the privacy of her room to let what just happened sink in, but she knew there would be trouble if she was late taking the kitchen leftovers to the pigsty.

∞ ∽

The next day, Saroya felt like she was living two lives. Her physical life was the harsh working reality of an indentured servant. The life spread before her in her mind was one of family and friends, where people did not look at her askance in the street. Where they did not look down on any Untalent, and the camps and forced round-ups were a thing of the past. Where the plague was a footnote in history, perhaps with her name next to a notation about the cure. She whacked the carpet in front of her with relish, imagining the look on Martezha's face when Urdig kicked her out of the castle.

The cloud of carpet dust still hovered about her head when Saroya spotted a tall woman gliding towards her. She recognized Isolte, the lady of the manor. Her aunt. Isolte halted well clear of the motes of grime.

"Come with me." She whirled in a flurry of brocaded skirts and headed back for the manor. Saroya dropped the stick she held and hurried after her. So much for this particular family reunion. Isolte exuded disdain.

Saroya discreetly brushed clinging bits of dirt from her tunic. She found herself in a part of the house that had been off-limits to her until now: the family quarters. Isolte passed through a polished walnut door and, following, Saroya entered a marble-tiled bathing room. A steaming tub of water occupied the centre of the room.

"Clean yourself off and then join me in my chambers." Isolte gestured to a door in the far wall. "Don't tarry. And wash your hair."

Once assured that Isolte had left the room, Saroya shed her clothes and stepped into the bath. Her skin shrank from the hot water. More accustomed to wiping herself down using a pitcher of cold water, she soon found herself luxuriating in the liquid embrace. She sank beneath the surface to moisten her hair then scrubbed herself vigorously. Tempted to soak for as long as the water kept its heat, she nevertheless hauled herself out of the tub as soon as she felt clean. It would not do to anger Isolte. She grabbed a clean robe, belted it about her waist, then, after towelling off her hair, stepped into Isolte's chambers.

Isolte stood by a window, tapping her foot. A dress and undergarments were laid out on the large four-poster bed. Isolte went to the bed and picked up some leggings. "You will dress. I will help you."

Saroya shrugged off the robe and reached for an undergarment. Isolte gasped. "What are those?"

Saroya had forgotten about the scabs that still fell away

from her body. She shrugged. "I had the plague." Isolte took a hasty step back. "I'm not sick anymore but it left me with these. I think they're going away." Saroya debated telling Isolte about the well at Abaya House but caution stilled her tongue. Everybody she told accused her of lying.

Saroya struggled into the unfamiliar clothes. She usually wore tunics and leggings, or simple dresses of rough wool or linen. The heavy brocades and silks over layers of undergarments nearly defeated her efforts to put them on. The sleeves of the brown underrobe clung to her arms. Isolte jerked the lacings tight on the corselet then did the same for the honey-coloured silk gown once Saroya wriggled into it. Saroya glanced down at her chest. The low, boat-shaped neckline exposed her shoulders and the top of the corselet; she wasn't used to seeing so much of her own skin. Isolte grimaced but Saroya knew nothing could be done about the sun-darkened square at her throat. No amount of scrubbing would fashionably lighten her complexion.

The bell-shaped sleeves of the gown fell away from her forearms, exposing the band of embroidery, golden against the brown, around the wrists of the underrobe. A winding pattern of scarlet leaves and vines trimmed the neckline, sleeves, and hem. The full skirts flared into a train behind her—she reminded herself to hold them up so she wouldn't trip. Isolte handed her an ornamented belt set with topaz and garnet-coloured glass beads, which, once set over her hips, hung below her waist. Saroya fingered the shoes next to the bed before she slipped them on. The kidskin felt like velvet.

Isolte snatched a comb from the bedside table and yanked it through Saroya's hair. Saroya winced as the teeth caught in several knots. Isolte did not have a gentle touch. By the time Isolte piled Saroya's hair into an elegant cascade, her scalp burned from the scratches of what felt like hundreds of pins. Her skin stretched tightly around her forehead, pulled back by Isolte's hair clips. When Isolte held up a mirror, Saroya was surprised to find no blood trickling down her neck from her hairline. She was sure Isolte punctured her at least once.

Catching sight of herself in the mirror, for once Saroya forgot to envy Nalini's straight hair. The person who stared back from the mirror seemed like a stranger. She looked almost … regal.

Isolte stopped fussing and stepped back to appraise her work.

"You'll do." She held out a fur-trimmed cloak. Despite the heat, Saroya tied it around her shoulders. "Come with me." Isolte led her down to the water arcade, where a polished black barque waited for them at the gate. Red- and gold-striped fabric draped over a frame shaded the cushioned seats.

"Where are we going?"

"To the palace. You will say nothing unless spoken to, and even then, you will keep your talk to a minimum. Loric will speak for you."

"Where is he?"

"He's meeting us at the castle. Put the hood on over your head. If things go wrong, there's no use in the whole house knowing about it."

Saroya settled herself onto a bench near the bow. This was not the welcome she had hoped from her family. Would her reception at the castle be different? Surely her father would show her some affection. Surely? Saroya tamped down that hope. No one except Veshwa had proven they'd cared. She got the distinct feeling her aunt and uncle viewed her as a playing piece in a game she didn't understand. Why should her father and uncle, Dhilain, be any different? The politics of nobility were beyond her. But she couldn't just dive off this barque now. Not in these heavy skirts. Saroya sighed. Hope for the best, but prepare for the worst. Which at this point was continued indenture to Loric.

The barquier poled his craft through the city. Isolte pressed her lips together in disapproval at what she saw outside.

"I told Loric we should have left U'Veyle last month. Now it's too late. Just look at those wretches."

Saroya stared out from behind the curtains at scenes of chaos. Body reclaimers tossed the dead onto small funeral barges. At each bridge they passed mothers pleading with city guards let them out of the city with their children. Saroya could only watch helplessly as the guards, shouting "Forged!", tore up one woman's proffered Talent certificate. They separated her from her two wailing children, and threw her into a cart Saroya knew was destined for a death camp.

The barque glided past the mouths of alleys, from which emanated the cries of street hawkers advertising every ineffective cure imaginable. The plague spread without check.

"They can't help being sick."

Isolte sniffed. "We shan't be able to help it either if we stay in this cesspool."

Saroya wondered if the papers she'd amassed in the Vergal still lay hidden at Balreg's pub. If everything went well today, she'd retrieve them, and put and end to the horrible pens for Untalents. She repressed a nervous twinge about the ring. Was her proof as ironclad as she hoped? She didn't trust Loric or Isolte.

The barquier navigated the canals with skill, moving them ever eastward through the maze of channels. Saroya lost herself admiring the hanging gardens and secret courtyards of the manors they floated past. Several times, she thought they might not clear a low bridge. The barquier seemed unperturbed. The great esplanade of the Grand Plaza teemed with pigeons and gulls. Saroya and Isolte disembarked at the castle basin. A waiting guard escorted them up the promenade stairs.

At the castle gate, they submitted to the inspection of a healer, who felt their foreheads for fever before allowing them through. Master Guffin met them in the courtyard. Saroya peered out at the steward from beneath her hood. He didn't appear to recognize her.

"My Lady Isolte," Guffin said. "Lord Dorn awaits you

and your guest in the reception hall. May I take your cloaks?" Saroya stifled in the late spring heat underneath her hood and would have accepted gratefully but Isolte shook her head.

"Later. Take us to the hall."

The reception hall? Saroya gripped the edge of her cloak. Something wasn't right.

CHAPTER 13

Saroya struggled to mask her surprise as she and Isolte entered the reception hall. She had expected a small gathering: the king, Martezha, and Lord and Lady Dorn. Instead, nobles packed the room. A murmur rippled across the crowd as Isolte removed her cloak and Saroya hesitantly followed suit. Her discomfort increased as she endured the stares of all these strangers. Was this not a private family matter? Suddenly the trap appeared clearly before her: Veshwa told her an Untalented daughter was dangerous to Urdig's reign—Loric and Isolte planned to use her against him.

Saroya lunged for the door but Isolte grabbed her hand and jerked her across the floor. Saroya spotted Loric conversing with the king. Loric's expression turned from boredom to satisfaction when he spied her in the crowd. He gestured to the king, and Urdig glanced in their direction. Martezha swept up to the two men, turning to see what drew their attention. She paled in shock at seeing Saroya in her finery then flushed an angry red. Isolte offered her husband a complicit smile, then curtsied in front of the king. Not knowing what else to do, Saroya imitated her.

Urdig waved them up. "Loric, you have brought me a new guest?"

"Your Majesty, may I present Saroya Bardan? I rescued her from a life of servitude and misery a week ago. I thought it important that you meet her."

The king looked puzzled, but before he could speak, Martezha, no longer able to contain herself, interrupted. "How dare you bring this mongrel to my father's court? Of course she was a servant. Not only is she a half-breed, she's an Untalent. I want her out of my sight." Several nobles moved away at the word "Untalent", as though fearing plague, while others drew closer to eavesdrop. Saroya ignored Martezha's slurs and mustered as much dignity as possible.

Urdig chided Martezha. "My dear, surely you do not wish to offend your uncle. Loric must have good reason ..." His eyes widened and his voice trailed off as he spotted the ring hanging around Saroya's neck. He reached for it but stopped short of touching her. "Where—where did you get that?"

Saroya looked him in the eye. "Your Majesty, may I speak with you in private?"

Loric was having none of it. "It was her mother's."

Urdig staggered as though struck. Eiden Callor, who stood nearby, moved to steady him. Martezha's lips trembled with rage. Loric directed an unpleasant smile toward her.

"Your Majesty, it would appear all this time you have been duped. You shelter an impostor. Mistress Bardan tells an interesting story about how Queen Padvai's other ring wound up in your supposed daughter's possession."

An excited babble rippled across the crowd. "The king, deceived in such a way ..." "Did you hear her, she said she was Untalented ..." Mortified, Saroya wished Loric would stop. While she was enjoying Martezha's comeuppance, this was not how she'd hoped to introduce herself to her father. What if he rejected her in front of all these people? How could she ever live down the shame? Or convince anyone afterwards that she knew how to stop the plague? She couldn't take her eyes off Urdig's confused face.

A sudden movement caught Saroya's peripheral vision. Martezha stepped in front of her and ripped the leather thong from her neck. "This is preposterous. I won't have it. Some servant shows up with another piece of jewelry and you believe her over me?"

Eiden Callor grabbed Martezha's wrist and pried the ring out of her clenched fingers. He then placed a hand upon the king's arm. "Your Majesty, we should adjourn to a quieter location." His significant look around the room snapped Urdig out of his paralysis.

"Yes, yes." He searched the crowd. "Guffin, fetch the ebony box on my dresser. Bring it to us in the library."

Saroya clutched her skirts as she moved with the small knot of people through several hallways. The men's boots echoed through the tiled halls like hammer blows. She felt small and uncertain between Loric and Isolte.

Once in the library, Eiden Callor shut the door behind them and stood guarding the exit. As Saroya passed him, Callor pressed the ring into her palm. "I believe this is yours." He did not sound happy.

Saroya took a seat in a leather-cushioned chair, avoiding the settee Isolte and Loric chose. Martezha paced the room, skirts swirling about her. Urdig approached Saroya's chair and stood before her.

"Now child, tell me how you come to have this ring."

Saroya swallowed then haltingly relayed her story—her days in Adram Vale, knowing she was an orphan, and the time when the Adepts gave her the first ring and parchment. She recounted the theft of the ring prior to leaving for U'Veyle, and her dismay when she discovered its significance. Martezha punctuated this news with disbelieving snorts.

Callor interrupted her monologue. "Majesty, Mistress Bardan approached me that evening. Her friend could not vouch that the ring taken from Martezha's bags was one and the same. I judged her a desperate girl, willing to tell any tale to better her lot. I felt it prudent not to bother you with her story. I see now that I was gravely mistaken. If you request it, I will submit my resignation."

Urdig grunted. "We will speak of the matter of your resignation later. Continue, Mistress Bardan."

Saroya drew breath and recounted how the note left for

her many years ago led her to search out Veshwa, who gave her the second ring.

"Do you still have this note?"

Saroya nodded, and rummaged in the pocket of her cloak for the well-worn piece of parchment wrapped in oilskin. Urdig examined it, but said nothing. A knock at the door provided a momentary distraction. Master Guffin walked in carrying a small, carved black box. The polished wood gleamed in the candlelight as the steward placed it on a table. King Urdig went to the table, opened the box and drew out a small square of folded velvet. He came back to Saroya and held out his hand.

"Give me your ring."

Saroya held out the thin strip of leather in a shaky hand. She dropped the ring into his palm.

"Don't worry, I'll give it back."

She nodded, a lump in her throat at the thought that he understood what it meant to her.

With great care, he unfolded the cloth and extracted a delicate twist of metal. He put the two rings together and they slotted into place, a perfect match.

He let out a slow breath then looked Saroya in the eyes. She hadn't realized she'd been holding her own breath. "Well, well." He glanced at Martezha. "The handwriting on the note is unmistakably Padvai's. I suppose you didn't steal it as well because you only had jewelry on your mind." She squeaked in protest. He turned to Callor. "Eiden, please escort Martezha to her quarters. She is not to leave the castle

until I say so. Send a delegation to Adram Vale. They are to
discover as much as they can about the backgrounds of
these two women. Our previous inquiries must not have
delved deeply enough."

Callor gripped Martezha just above the elbow and
handed her over to Master Guffin, who led her from the
room. Saroya could hear her shrill protestations all the way
down the hall. Urdig turned to Loric. "It would seem, Lord
Dorn, that I will eventually have to thank you for returning
my daughter to me."

Loric inclined his head. "Eventually?"

"The matter is too sensitive to confirm without further
investigation. I will wait until the delegation returns from
Adram Vale. In the meantime, Martezha will remain out of
sight. Mistress Bardan as well. Rumours must be spreading
like wildfire as it is." Isolte whispered in Loric's ear.

"My Lord, if you do not wish to acknowledge Mistress
Bardan at this time, my wife and I will offer her the
hospitality of our home until the matter is resolved."

Eiden Callor start to protest and Saroya opened her
mouth to chime in, but Loric forestalled her. He stared
down Callor.

"My wife is most upset at the past treatment her niece
received here. We will give her the courtesy she deserves."

Urdig considered Loric then shrugged. "The Houses may
interpret her staying in the castle as an implicit
acknowledgement. Very well. We will do it your way."

"But—!" Saroya tried to object—to be so close only to

226 ~ KATRINA ARCHER

get sent away again!—but Loric grabbed her arm. She would bruise tomorrow where his grip tightened. Her misgivings about trusting him deepened.

"Come along, my dear. It's best if we do things by the book," Loric said.

Before she could say anything else or even mention the plague, Loric bowed and led Isolte and Saroya from the room.

∾ ∽

Saroya stood in Loric's study, refusing the offer of a chair. Loric, arms clasped behind his back, stared out one of the long windows. She had never seen his study before, although she had passed by several times during the course of her duties. Dark walnut panelling created a somber mood, enhanced by displays of ancient fighting weapons. An ornate desk faced a large fireplace. Resting a hand on the desk for support, she cleared her throat. He spun around.

"My Lord Dorn, I apologize for coming unannounced." Though she really felt far from sorry. He'd used her. Now Saroya understood a bit better how Nalini felt when Saroya used Goha Ferlen's name for her own aims. Her outraged simmered on a slow burn.

"How can I help you?" His tone did not match his words, and Saroya stiffened.

There was no point dancing around the issue. "Was it necessary to expose me so publicly? I would have preferred a private audience—as it is, rumours are flying, Martezha is throwing fits that can be heard clear down the coast, and the castle is in a complete uproar."

"I give you everything you ever wanted and you dare question my methods? Come now, child, what does it matter how I chose to reveal you?"

Saroya swallowed her fear of what he might do to her. He was a powerful bully, yes, but still just a bully. He thought to keep her yoked to him. She had other ideas. "You know exactly how much it matters. Next we'll be hearing calls for Urdig's abdication."

Loric's smile was ugly. "If my ambitions are met at the same time as yours, we both win, don't we? Surely you don't believe my generosity should go unrewarded? I will determine those rewards, not you. Isolte tells me you had the plague."

Saroya grew even more wary at the change of subject. "What of it?"

"Tell me how you got better."

"Some kind women at an almshouse nursed me back to health."

"Which almshouse?"

"What does it matter?"

He lunged at her and she found herself trapped between him and the desk. She shrank back. "People are dying. Yet you live. If I know who these 'kind women' are, I can persuade them to share their healing prowess with the kingdom."

Saroya tried to hold his gaze but failed. Her eyes drifted

down to the desk. She clutched the edge of the desk in surprise. Loric interposed a hand too late to hide the object that held her breathless in shock. She snatched it before he could sweep it into a pocket and held it in front of his nose. It was a twisted ring of metal, a matching peer to the one around her neck and the one at the castle, right down to the amethyst colour and size of the inset stones.

"Where did you get this?" Her hand trembled.

Loric feigned nonchalance. He sauntered over to the door and closed it. "Do you really want to know? Think carefully, now."

Saroya could hardly breathe. She had never seen any other jewelry quite like the ring on the leather thong around her neck. The ring at the castle matched exactly—the two fit like a mated set, although they did not hold together. Looking at this piece, she could imagine how the three would interlock like the parts of a puzzle.

Loric's insidious voice continued on, mocking her. "The ring at the castle was Padvai's most prized possession, by all accounts. To her second most prized possession, you, she gave its twin."

"But why would she give you—?"

Loric smiled. A doubt niggled at the back of Saroya's brain. She looked down at the ring. Back up into Loric's grey eyes. His upturned lips. Understanding rushed in. She'd seen those eyes reflected back at her in mirrors and pools her whole life. She sank down into the leather chair next to the desk.

"Not Urdig."

"No. Not Urdig."

A wave of nausea swept up her throat.

"You've known all along." Every word she said sounded stupid and naïve to her ears.

"That Padvai's child was also mine, yes. That you specifically were that child, no. Martezha is certainly ambitious enough to come from my side of the family."

"Why haven't you said anything?"

He sneered at her. "What, and let the world know I fathered a worthless bastard? No, you're much more useful to me exactly as the world perceives you now. Now tell me how you beat the plague."

My mother slept with Loric? Betrayed both her husband and her sister? Saroya's world shrank to a small, miserable point. Blinded, she dropped the ring on the floor. It tinkled as it bounced underneath the desk. He despised her. He was only interested in using her to achieve the throne. She wasn't even a person to him, just a means to an end.

"I'll tell him."

Looming in front of her, Loric grabbed her by the chin. The pressure of his fingers hurt her jaw. A wave of revulsion swept through her at his touch.

"I don't think so."

She glared up at him, anger seething through her shock.

"It won't save his throne. Either he's fathered an Untalent or he's been cuckolded. Either is enough of a scandal to bring him down, now that the plague weakened his popularity. Keep your silence and you'll live in comfort for the rest of your life. Betray me and you'll stay bonded. And I won't keep you here in the manor. I'll ship you off somewhere distinctly less pleasant, I assure you." He shook her head roughly before releasing her. She lost her balance and fell to her hands and knees. "Do we understand each other?"

Saroya nodded. Then, before he could react, she darted from the room. Loric shouted behind her, but she nipped down a servant's short cut and lost him. She cared not if the servants of House Dorn witnessed her escape. Once free of the house and grounds, she hid, shivering, behind a hedge until the clatter of hooves told her Loric's men had passed her by. Then she slunk through the streets of the Manor District, avoiding horsemen, until she reached the Dalcen Canal and could see the castle. Yet even the castle was no longer a safe haven. There was nowhere to hide from the truth.

CHAPTER 14

"How could you lose her?"

Loric resented Daravela's tone. "A small matter. One I shall soon put to rights."

Daravela sniffed. "What was she wearing?"

Loric described Saroya then continued. "I didn't come here to discuss minor setbacks, Eminence. I thought you should know—the plague is curable."

Daravela set down the letter sealer she had been toying with and gave Loric her full attention. "Were that true, it would be most welcome news indeed. In the right hands, of course."

"That is why I hastened here, Eminence. The girl caught the plague, but didn't die from it. She claims she received the cure in a Vergal almshouse."

"And you don't know which one."

Loric did not rise to Daravela's jab. "That is where the Order comes in. I'm sure you wield considerable influence with the Healer's Guild."

Daravela concurred.

"Then you also agree that Urdig must not be the first to announce this news?" Loric asked.

"I'll speak to the healers." Daravela summoned her assistant. "Fetch the heads of all the guilds. And the chief magistrate. I need a search conducted."

Loric relaxed. The girl couldn't possibly escape an all-out search by the magistrates.

∞ ∽

In the distance, Saroya could just make out the arch of the bridge where she'd spent so many cold and miserable nights. She'd tried to get to the Healer's Guild in the Market District, in the faint hope that Nalini might help her, but a magistrate stood at the foot of the span crossing the Aghrab River. Even though she still wore her fine silks, he'd stared at her suspiciously. Uneasy, she turned away. Did Loric have enough power to set the magistrates looking for her?

The small stone bridge that had been her home seemed like the next best place to wait out the night. She neared the gap in the stone that allowed her to get underneath, but a magistrate stepped out of an alley. Instinctively, Saroya turned in the opposite direction, but bumped into two grey-robed Adepts.

"Excuse me," Saroya said. The Adept on the right started to bow, mistaking Saroya for a noble, then his eyes widened. He grabbed Saroya's arm, shouting for the magistrate.

"It's her! It's her!"

Before Saroya knew what was happening, someone thrust a burlap bag over her head. She kicked and screamed, but rough hands tied her arms behind her back and a man heaved her into the bed of a barque then sat on her. Saroya couldn't breathe, much less fight back.

The terrible pressure on her chest only eased when the barque pulled up to a water gate. The magistrate dumped Saroya out of the barque then led her through a doorway. She splashed through puddles left by the high tide, her stumbling footsteps echoing off the stones arching overhead. Her captor yanked her up several flights of stairs, before leading her into a quiet room. Saroya tripped on the edge of a carpet before he pushed her down into a chair. He unbound her hands and ripped the hood off her head. Saroya blinked in the sudden light and resisted the urge to scratch at her nose where the burlap made it itchy. The magistrate exited the room, leaving Saroya alone with its only other occupant.

"Do you know who I am, child?"

Saroya stared at the wrinkled old woman behind the desk. The massive block of wood made her look tiny, as though she had shrunk like a wool blanket accidentally washed in hot water. The woman wore a plain grey robe. An Adept. Saroya kept her counsel. She was tired of strangers calling her a child.

"My name is Daravela. You may call me Eminence."

Saroya stayed silent. What did the Order of Adepts want

with her? Jail and a return to her bond, she could understand. But an audience with the head of the Order?

The woman fanned out a sheaf of parchments. "You have an interesting family history."

Saroya swallowed. Daravela drummed her fingers on the parchment. Claws. Saroya could think of nothing else as she gazed hypnotized at the liver-spotted skin stretched tight around the woman's knuckles. How much did Daravela know?

"Tell me, why did Padvai hide you?"

"I don't understand."

Daravela's hand came down on the desk with surprising force. Saroya jumped. "Don't take me for a fool. I know you were at the castle today."

"I'm Untalented."

"House Roshan knows how to disguise its Untalents. You're more dangerous left in place."

Dangerous? Saroya shook her head.

"An Untalent on the throne would have been Roshan's crowning glory. Why did Padvai send you away?"

Saroya clamped her mouth shut, the wound of Loric's rejection too fresh in her mind.

A knock at the door interrupted the interrogation. Daravela shot an irritated glance at Saroya then shuffled out of the room. Saroya heard a latch lock behind her. She couldn't see another exit. She stood up to check out the window, but the parchments on the desk captured her attention. She riffled through them. They appeared to be old

Testing results, all for House Roshan. Her own name scrawled across the top of a sheet caught her eye. Saroya scanned her results. That couldn't be right ...

The clunk of the latch startled Saroya and she turned the paper around so that it appeared untouched, before scurrying back to the chair. Her heart pounded against her ribcage. Daravela eased herself back into the chair behind the desk.

"Very well. Perhaps you actually don't know. You can demonstrate your good will by telling me how you overcame the plague."

Caution flooded Saroya. Only Loric could have told the eminence about Saroya's recovery. Daravela sought to use her as well.

"Am I a prisoner?"

"Answer my question and you are free to return to Lord Dorn."

"That just trades one prison for another."

"How did you heal yourself?"

"I'm an Untalent, not a healer. How should I know?"

"You fancied yourself a healer once."

"And I'm paying the price."

"The plague cure, child. Tell me. We fed, clothed, and educated you for years. You owe the Order a life debt."

Saroya shot out of her chair. "I owe you nothing. Nothing!" *Least of all the truth.* "You ruined my life."

"We only told you what you were."

"No. You denied what I am." Saroya snatched up her

Testing paper, waving it in Daravela's face. "I only got two questions wrong on the Testing!"

Daravela froze. "You had no business—"

"This says I can be a healer. A builder. Or a merchant. Anything!"

"A Talent must show a clear predilection—"

"Predilection? What about skill?" Saroya leaned over the desk. At her Testing, Doyenne Ganarra had said "too scattered". It hadn't meant wrong. Had never meant wrong. Daravela recoiled, while tumblers clicked into place in Saroya's head.

"You're afraid of me." Afraid of losing her power. Saroya felt sick with the knowledge crashing in on her: the Order of Adepts stoked the people's hatred of Untalents. Daravela fed the fears of the masses so that Untalents would stay weak and never rise up against the Order.

It was Daravela's turn to stay silent.

"I'm not Untalented. I'm something else. And that frightens you."

"You are whatever the Order says you are." Daravela eyes bored into Saroya's as she grabbed the parchment from Saroya's hand.

Saroya got a hold of herself. She needed to humour this woman until she could figure out how to escape. Saroya slumped back in her chair, trying to look cowed. A plan took shape in her mind. "I'll take you to the almshouse."

Saroya led the party of Adepts to the almshouse where she'd encountered the madman. Daravela stared in disgust at the burned remains in the courtyard.

"They were alive when I left," Saroya said.

"Liar. This is the wrong place."

"They fed me broth. Maybe you'll find something in their stores."

Daravela ordered the four other Adepts to search the almshouse. When they disappeared into the building, Saroya turned to Daravela.

"I'm leaving. I'll give your regards to Loric."

"You'll stay right here until we find the cure." Daravela clutched at Saroya's arm but Saroya shook off the frail woman easily.

"The king won't take kindly to the Order kidnapping his daughter."

Daravela's eyes narrowed but she kept her hands off Saroya. "As kindly as he took to the news of an Untalented daughter? The cure—what is it?"

"Why Eminence—it almost sounds as though you need me. But that can't be true. Untalents are useless." Saroya laughed.

She walked out the door. Nobody stopped her. Apparently Daravela wasn't prepared to call her bluff.

∞ ∞

"Lord Dorn's hospitality not to your taste?"

Saroya shrugged. Eiden Callor did not seem happy to see her. When she'd knocked on the barracks gate, the watch captain happened to be the same one she'd spoken to on her first visit; he took her straight to Callor.

"I need to go to the Vergal."

"Then go."

"I need some authority to back me up."

Callor waited for her to elaborate.

"When I was there, I discovered several things that might help fight the plague's spread. The Healer's Guild wouldn't listen to me, though, because of what I'd done."

"Done?"

She explained about posing as a healer. "The guild was right to punish me."

"What discoveries?"

"I need to go back to the Vergal to get my notes on how the plague spread. A well at an almshouse might hold the key to a cure, but I'd need to visit again to be sure."

"Why do you need me?"

"Madam Abaya won't let me back in until the plague is over. But maybe with a king's man ..."

"The Vergal's too dangerous."

"Not for me. I've had the fever. I don't think it can hurt me anymore."

"You survived the plague?" Callor shook his head. "If the healers can't fight it, what makes you believe you weren't simply lucky?"

"It's precisely because I'm not a healer that I can help." And suddenly, she knew it in her core for the deepest truth she'd spoken in months. "The healers are too focused on a single idea—the fouled air. They can't see beyond their assumptions. I can."

Callor looked doubtful.

"Please. Let me show you that I'm more than what everyone says I am."

∽ ↄ

Isolte stared at the ruin of Loric's study. When she'd heard the first crash, she debated not investigating, but matters were coming to a head and she needed to know any bad news. She stood in the door, watching Loric sweep everything from his desk in one motion. A porcelain vase from Kurtya shattered into tiny pieces on the floor, joining splinters of wood from a smashed chair, a tattered portrait and sundry other now unidentifiable objects. Just when she thought he'd calmed down, he reached into his pocket and hurled a small object out the window. She heard a faint clink as it hit the paving stones.

"Loric, what—"

"She ran. That idiot I hired to watch the grounds let her escape and she gave my horsemen the slip."

"What did you say to her?"

He shrugged.

"You'll find her—"

"What if she heads for the castle, Isolte?"

"Then we have nothing to worry about."

"She didn't tell me how she survived the plague. It's critical—critical!—that I be the one to bring that information before the Houses." He kicked at a sheathed sword lying on the floor.

"What will you do?"

"I have some almshouses in the Vergal to look into."

∾ ∾

That evening Saroya found herself on horseback for the first time since arriving in U'Veyle. The girl who'd entered the big city with such modest hopes seemed like a different person. Now, she had to save that city. Eiden Callor rode a tall bay gelding next to her. His frigid demeanor had not softened since they met in the courtyard and mounted for their journey to the Vergal. Shrouded as they were in plague masks, she could not make out more of his expression beyond a disapproving glare. They approached the Spotted Salmon with nothing but the clatter of the horses' hooves and moaning pleas of ill beggars interrupting the silence. Saroya had had enough.

"Captain Callor, please tell me what's wrong."

He dismounted in front of the pub and hitched both their horses while she clambered less gracefully down from her own mount.

"The Vergal is not my favourite destination."

They entered the pub, and Saroya was pleased to see nothing had been touched. At least Balreg might return to find his business still intact. "That's not the only thing. You've been angry with me since earlier."

He rounded on her. "Do you not see what you've done?"

"I did what I had to. Had you been in my place, watching

someone else steal your life, wouldn't you have done the same?"

"You've taken down Urdig in the process. I could forgive a lot, but not that."

She couldn't look at him.

"The noble Houses are already muttering about forcing him to abdicate. They don't want to see anyone on the throne who sired an Untalent. You played straight into Loric's hands. He's set the stage for months, spreading discontent about the handling of the plague, fomenting anger at paying Untalents even for servile jobs, blaming them for the plague—all the while quietly ensuring that the nobles know who would handle each of these issues in the 'proper' manner. Didn't you know this?"

"How could I be expected to know? I've been living on the street! Do you think I bothered with the doings of the Great Circle of Houses while I dug through trash for my meals?" Saroya dug her fingers into her palm, trying to calm down. "Doesn't it distress you that a fraud has been taking advantage of him for almost a year? Because that's what Martezha is, singing Talent or not. She never cared much for Urdig. Only what he could do for her."

"How are you different? You go from being a reviled servant to a rich noble. You damage his chances of keeping his throne. Why should I believe that you care a whit for him?"

They had climbed to the second floor and Saroya now pried back the floorboard underneath which she hid all her parchment notes from her canvassing of the Vergal. She pulled them out and attached the spare pouch to her belt.

"If the nobles want him off the throne because I'm Untalented, there's nothing I can do. But maybe I can help him deal with the plague. Loric and Daravela both wanted me to tell them the thing I'm about to show you. Watch me and judge for yourself."

She marched back down the stairs and untangled the reins of her horse. She only waited long enough to make sure that Callor followed before kicking her horse into a trot and heading for Abaya House.

The same plump woman answered Saroya's impatient ring of the bell.

"No visitors. The plague, you know."

Saroya raised her plague shroud. "Do you remember me? I came a few days back?"

The woman nodded.

"I must speak with Madam Abaya. Please fetch her. It's urgent."

The woman waddled off, moving as quickly as her bulk would allow. In short order, Madam Abaya faced them, hands on her hips.

"We had an agreement. You would not come back here until after the plague is gone. I can't allow you back to visit Veshwa."

"We're not here to see Veshwa. This is Eiden Callor, captain of the King's Guards. Are your grounds still free of plague?"

"Yes. Which is precisely why you're not coming in."

"There's more than isolation protecting you from the fevers."

"I'm afraid I don't follow."

"Most people in U'Veyle get their drinking water from the aqueducts. Here, you all drink from that well, and you're all plague-free. I'd like to examine your well."

Saroya was sure Madam Abaya would turn them away. Eiden Callor leaned forward in his saddle.

"Madam Abaya, I'm sure you would not refuse a personal request from King Urdig. We took the greatest precautions. We spoke to no one since leaving the castle and promise to remain outside the building. I vouch that we are both free of fever."

"That's what she said last time." With obvious reluctance, Madam Abaya drew out a key from a pocket in her skirt and unlocked the gate. "Please follow me."

Saroya untied two large water skins from her saddle and asked Callor to do the same. She knew her request to bring them along this morning puzzled him. She slung hers over her shoulder then followed Madam Abaya into the courtyard. She and Callor waited on the bench while Madam Abaya fetched an aide. The well looked much like any other well Saroya had seen: grey stone with a bucket hanging from a hand-turned axle. The only unusual feature was the mass of lichen growing over the rock, so much that one could barely make out the colour of the stone.

Madam Abaya returned, a young woman trailing behind

her. "Please fill the water skins," Saroya instructed her. "I'll need a sample of the lichen, too." While Callor helped the young woman with the water, Madam Abaya trimmed a small pile of the lichen from the stone. Saroya stuffed this into her belt pouch. When the water skins were full, Madam Abaya dismissed the girl.

"What now?" Madam Abaya asked Saroya.

"I take what you've given me to the healers."

"And if you are incorrect? I've never liked our dependence on the well—everyone knows the fountain water is purer."

"If I'm wrong, then your well is the least of your worries. Thank you for allowing us this much. All of U'Veyle may be in your debt."

Madam Abaya arched a sceptical eyebrow. "If that is true, we shall share as much as we are able. Good day to you."

Saroya and Callor took their leave and rode to the Healer's Guild. Callor took her to the back of the guild building, using the same entrance she'd last exited as a bonded criminal. She asked the clerk on duty to find Nalini. When her friend hurried into the courtyard, her puzzled expression changed to one of distrust.

"Why are you here? What's going on?" She shot a wary glance at Callor. "What happened to your bond?"

Saroya drew her away from the inquisitive clerk. "I can't explain about the bond right now. Suffice it to say that certain people now know who's a thief and who isn't."

Despite herself, Nalini grinned. "But I'm not here about that, and you mustn't mention it to anyone."

"What, then?"

"Take these water skins. It's probably best if the guild doesn't find out who brought them. Tell them Captain Callor brought them." Saroya handed Nalini a parchment with the exact location of Madam Abaya's well. "No one who drinks water from this well gets sick."

Nalini eyed the waterbags, interest overcoming hostility. "There's a good reason most cooks won't use well or cistern water to prepare food. It's stagnant. What makes this well special?"

Saroya pulled the harvested lichen from her belt pouch. "This was growing all over it. I was never the best herbologist in agronomy class, but I have a good memory and don't remember seeing anything like it. You'd know better. You should dry it out and do all that other good healer stuff with it and see if in powder form it's as effective as the water."

"You're awfully confident about that water."

Saroya grinned. "No reason not to be. Test it and see. I came down with the plague there, and I survived."

Nalini's eyes narrowed. "You're lying again." She looked up at Callor, who shook his head.

Saroya continued. "I tried to tell you before. Nobody will listen to an Untalent, and it's important that if this is a cure, it gets used. Got it?"

"Right." Nalini waved down another healer and Callor

passed them the heavy water skins. "Where are you staying?"

Callor interjected. "Come find me if you wish to speak with Mistress Bardan." Nalini nodded, then made off with her bounty without another word. Saroya sighed. Maybe the gift of the cure wasn't enough to repair their friendship. Maybe nothing ever would be enough. Regardless of how things worked out for her at the castle, at least now the city would have a weapon against the plague.

Callor and Saroya headed back to the castle. When they approached the Grand Plaza and the boulevard that led to the Manor District, Saroya reined in her horse. "I'd rather not return to Manor Dorn."

Disapproval darkened Callor's gaze.

"I can't have the Houses thinking you've been acknowledged. I'll have Guffin find you an out-of-the-way room. But if I find out you've plotted to Urdig's disadvantage, you'll deal with me."

He jerked his own mount's reins and trotted away, shoulders rigid. Saroya followed, no longer sure of herself.

∞ ∽

Isolte did not look up as Loric shut the door to their bedchamber. She stared at something cradled in her palm. He shrugged off his jacket, sat down on the opposite side of the bed and bent over to pull off his boots.

"Things are looking up. The Adepts found the Vergal almshouse and the plague riots should reach boiling point in short order."

He heard Isolte's skirts rustle as she stood up.

"Have you loved her all this time?"

Loric froze. "The girl? Don't be stupid."

"The only stupid thing I ever did was marry you."

"What's gotten into you? Worried my affections are wandering? You're the mother of my child."

"And so is she, isn't she?"

Loric twisted around to face his wife. Isolte glared, white faced and rigid. A tiny muscle above her jaw twitched.

"Nonsense. She's barely more than a child herself," Loric said.

"Enough! You know I don't mean Saroya."

"Then who? Whatever game you're playing, Isolte, my patience is wearing thin."

"You know exactly who."

"I'm sure I don't."

"Then where did you get this?" She whipped her arm towards him and something hard hit his cheek before bouncing onto the coverlet. He stretched out a finger and nudged the gold band of the puzzle ring.

"It was always Padvai, wasn't it?" Isolte said.

Loric shrugged.

"I made your estates successful. It was my Talent—mine! —that restored your family's riches after you gambled them away. You'd be nothing without me. This is how you repay me? By fathering a bastard by that slut? That whore?"

Loric stood up from the bed, walked up to Isolte with a measured stride, and struck her hard across the cheek.

"She was never meant for Urdig. But she would not go against your father's wishes. Even after Airic was dead, she wouldn't leave Urdig."

"I was never good enough for you."

"If Airic faked her certificate of Talent, neither was she. I suppose he did me a favour by giving her to Urdig."

Isolte was practically spitting. "You're the one who was never good enough. My father would never give his pet Padvai to a failed Talent."

Loric smacked her again. She brushed away a smear of blood from her lip.

"She might have loved you before but it was all over after she learned of your failure. What was Saroya's conception, then? Did she bed you out of pity?"

Loric refused to admit that to himself. He walked from the room, but couldn't resist loosing a weak parting arrow. "If I'm such a miserable failure, why did your father give you to me?"

Isolte shrieked as he slammed the door behind him.

∞ ∞

For two days, Saroya took all her meals in her room, avoiding company and ignoring knocks at the door. She told the maid Urdig provided her that she was not to be disturbed. She spent most of her time seated at the window in her room, staring at the distant mountain range and wondering if she would have been better off working for the village council in Adram Vale.

The dull ache of rejection filled her body like a physical wound. Since being ruled an Untalent, she had fought hard to prove otherwise, with the hope that her family would accept her in the end. That hope lay in ruins back at Manor Dorn.

No matter how confident Saroya tried to appear before Daravela, she couldn't avoid the truth: if the Order said Saroya was Untalented, the world would always see her that way. Her Testing results confused her. How could being so right be so wrong? The unfairness galled her. Suddenly Saroya saw every single other Untalent in a different light. How much potential was being wasted, how many other lives ruined? Or were Daravela and the doyenne right? Was she simply too unfocused to ever be great at any Talent? Lying to herself about her abilities only seemed to get people hurt.

It was now past dark and Saroya roused herself out of her introspection, her legs stiff from being cooped up in the room for so long. She had a decision to make and a short walk would clear her head. She shrugged on a tunic and made her way to the castle gardens overlooking the lagoon, avoiding the curious glances of the servants she encountered in the corridors.

She sank down onto the cool stone of a marble bench and inhaled the garden air. The flowery scent wafting in the sea breeze offered a refreshing change from the closed stuffiness of her room, but it failed to clear out the muddle in her head. She was about to give up and head back to her room when a rustle in the shrubs lining the path caught her ear. She looked up as Martezha paused in midstride. Saroya stifled a groan. The last thing she needed now was another of Martezha's strident attacks. She stood up to leave, hoping to avoid a confrontation.

To her considerable surprise, instead of flying off the handle, Martezha motioned her to sit back down. Saroya kept herself ready for a quick exit.

"You must hate me," Martezha said.

Saroya held her tongue and waited. Martezha licked her lips.

"I've told the king that he needn't wait for the delegation to return from Adram Vale. I'm quite sure either they or your uncle will report that Martezha Baghore was left at the Cloister by a couple called Idira and Aildeg Baghore."

Saroya sniffed. *Of course you're sure.* She continued to stare, not willing to let Martezha off the hook.

"I hated you. When I found out about you, I mean. My parents, they're like you. Untalents. I was so angry with them. They left me—they worried the stigma would rub off." Martezha smiled bitterly. "When I found out ... The taint would have ruined my singing career. I didn't know what the ring meant when I stole it. I just wanted to hurt you—get back at them, at any Untalent, somehow. Then when we came here, it seemed like the best way to erase them from everybody's memory. To let everybody think I was really the king's daughter."

"Why are you telling me this?"

Martezha shrugged. "It's over, and the truth is about to come out anyway. You and your kind—I'll never get used to coming from stock like that." Her lip curled. "But I'll have to live with myself. I think a part of me couldn't live with what I did, because I stopped being able to sing. Best you hear the truth from me."

"Are you asking me for forgiveness?"

"No. Why should you profit over me? It was just an accident of birth that you weren't their daughter. To me— you became their daughter."

Saroya didn't know whether to laugh or cry. Martezha— selfish and absorbed to the last.

∞ ∽

In the morning Saroya found a warm bowl of oatmeal in her chamber's anteroom. The two spoonfuls she managed to force down tasted like chalk. She heard a sharp rap on the door, and assumed it was someone come to take away the dirty dishes. She was not pleased to greet Eiden Callor instead. She shut the door in his face but he stuck out his arm.

"I'm not seeing anyone."

"You'll see me." He strode into the room and turned to face her. "Now—Guffin tells me you've been hiding here since we returned from the Vergal. Being discreet is one thing, but something's troubling you and you will tell me what."

"Guffin's wrong."

He grabbed her by the arm and she winced. "I will not see Urdig harmed by you or by Loric. Something happened between you. You haven't been sleeping."

She ripped her arm out of his grasp. She felt sick, and reached for the edge of a small table to steady herself. Few people left in her world had the slightest faith in her. Difficult to win over, in the end he helped her when it counted. So many lies. And none of them did her any good. Her walls crumbled and she sagged to her knees on the carpet.

"I don't know what to do." Her voice sounded alien to her.

He knelt in front of her and clasped her hand. "Tell me." Callor's voice was gentle now.

Saroya shook her head, angry at herself, at how she'd let herself be manipulated by Loric. "Nothing I tell you will help save Urdig. It would have been better for him if you'd never allowed me to follow you to U'Veyle."

"It's too late to worry about that now. What happened with Loric?"

Saroya's voice quavered. "Well, the good news is that Padvai really is my mother. The bad news is that Urdig isn't my father."

He gripped her hand tighter. "Who?"

She couldn't look at him anymore. "Loric," she whispered.

CHAPTER 15

Eiden Callor rocked back onto his heels, but didn't let go of Saroya's hand. Everything spilled out: Loric's possession of a matching ring, his threats against her and Urdig if she told anyone, his rationalization as to why she should keep silent.

"So why did you tell me?" Callor asked.

"Martezha lived a lie—where did it get her? People look at me like I'm vermin. Even—even you do. What would those looks be like if it all came out a year from now? I couldn't bear it. Loric could still change his mind if the wind blows the wrong way for him. I'm done with lying, with being something I'm not."

Eiden stood up. He pulled her to her feet, and when he drew away, she felt bereft.

"What happens now?" she asked.

"I have to tell Urdig, but we must keep this quiet or we risk alerting Loric." His expression was grim. "You mustn't speak to anyone, including your friend Nalini. Stay in your room. I'll send for you when I have news."

Two interminable days later a page summoned her to Urdig's private chambers. There, she found the king, Eiden Callor, and a tall ginger-haired man who looked familiar. She dropped into a deep curtsy.

Urdig released her from her obeisance, then introduced her to the man standing next to Callor. "Saroya, this is Dhilain of Roshan. My wife's brother."

Of course—he probably looked familiar because she'd caught a glimpse of him that evening long ago at Manor Roshan. This was the man Veshwa told her to seek out, before events caught her up in a whirlwind grip. Urdig spoke.

"Eiden Callor told us what you told him. We know what it must have cost you, and appreciate your honesty."

Saroya marvelled that this man, still recovering from the shock of his wife's betrayal, could be so gracious. Urdig continued.

"Loric placed both of us in difficult positions." Some deep emotion altered his voice. "When it became obvious, after many years together, that we could not conceive, I told Padvai that any child she bore I would treat as my own." Saroya's eyes widened. "Unfortunately, she chose as father the most ambitious and unpleasant man in the Kingdom of Veyle." A wry smile twisted his lips.

"Before these witnesses, I acknowledge you as Padvai's daughter. That said, nobody beyond these walls can ever know." He raised a hand to forestall her questions. "We spoke to Veshwa. She is a loyal servant and will tell no one the truth."

"Surely it's too late not to acknowledge me publicly? Loric knows about the ring."

"We'll have to stonewall him. Our word against his. He's called for a conclave of the Houses."

"Now?"

"Rumour has it he will formally call for my abdication. We shall address his charges together. Say nothing during the conclave. Dhilain and I will handle Loric."

Saroya faced Callor. "What about the healers?" She saw from Urdig's expression that he knew what she was asking about.

Callor shook his head. "Haven't heard back yet. Strange."

Urdig raised an eyebrow. "Her Eminence Daravela requested the honour of attending the conclave."

"Adept interference?" Callor asked.

"Perhaps. Time for you to fetch our insurance, I think," Urdig said. Callor nodded and left the room.

Urdig addressed Saroya. "Do you have the ring?"

Saroya touched the thong around her neck. She suspected simple denial would not stop Loric.

"Very well. Please follow me."

As Saroya trailed after Urdig and Dhilain into the hallway an idea occurred to her. She stopped short. When the men turned to see what was the matter, she took a deep breath—her future rested on whether she could convince them it was worth a try.

∾ ∾

Saroya tried not to fidget in her chair. The Hall of
Nobles, though grander, felt now to her much like the
Healer's Guild trial chamber. From her seat in the guest box,
she faced the nobles assembled in the circular room, noting
their curious stares. Those who had not been present when
Loric made his initial claim studied her. Some appeared
hostile, others smug. Urdig held court partway down the
room to her right on the royal dais, Dhilain across the room
in House Roshan's customary seat. Eiden Callor entered
with an unhappy Martezha towards the back of the dais. A
group of blue-sashed healers clustered in a viewing box,
deferring to a silver-haired woman resplendent in the gold-
embroidered grey robes of a senior Adept: Eminence
Daravela. Isolte sat stiffly next to Loric in House Dorn's
box, accompanied by a couple dressed in the slate grey of
indentured peasants.

A chamberlain strode to the edge of the dais. "All rise for
the royal anthem."

Urdig turned to Martezha. "Martezha, if you would be so
kind."

Martezha appeared surprised, but took up a position at
the front of the dais. For a moment, as she focused on the
floor, she looked sick, but then raised her head and stared
straight at the House Dorn box, and the people next to
Loric. Long seconds passed, and Saroya thought Martezha

might flee, but then her grim expression changed. Martezha closed her eyes, inhaled then launched into the most heartfelt rendition of the royal anthem Saroya had ever heard. Her beautiful clear tones floated throughout the Hall of Nobles.

Silence greeted the last lingering note. Martezha smiled then retired to the back of the dais. Saroya had never seen her so relaxed.

Loric approached the petitioner's pulpit.

"My fellow lords, I requested this extraordinary session of the Great Circle of Houses to bring happy news. Unfortunately, duty prevails upon me a most unpleasant task as well." Before Urdig could answer, Loric swept an arm round towards his box. "The healers bring great tidings—a cure for the plague!"

A cheer erupted throughout the hall. Saroya's heart sank. How had Loric managed to take credit for her discovery?

Urdig stood and called for calm. "A cure? Why wasn't I told first?" He glared at the master healer who was already making his way to the pulpit. The master healer bowed deeply.

"Apologies, Majesty. We have been working day and night testing a plant found only in the Vergal. When we feed it to plague patients, their fever abates, the sores disappear, and within a few days they are up and walking again, completely recovered. It is astounding."

"What sort of plant?"

"A lichen, Your Majesty. It grows on the stones of an

almshouse well in the Vergal."

Urdig turned to Callor. "Send guards to this almshouse. When word gets out, they will be mobbed, and we cannot risk losing this plant. Master Healer, my congratulations. Your guild has proven its worth yet again. All U'Veyle owes you a great debt of gratitude."

The healer inclined his head, an ingratiating smile on his face. "Were it not for Lord Dorn, Your Majesty ... Lord Dorn apprised Her Eminence of the existence of a pocket of people free of disease, which brought the plant to our attention."

Loric tried to appear modest, but Saroya saw right through him. Urdig cleared his throat. "Well, then, it appears Veyle also owes the same gratitude to House Dorn. And to the Adepts."

Eminence Daravela stood in the box, her voice carrying across the hall despite her tiny stooped frame. "It was the Order's duty to investigate."

Saroya clenched her fists. Loric and Daravela must have sent men to every single almshouse in the Vergal after she left. They tricked Madam Abaya into telling them about the well. But what happened to Nalini? Saroya glared at the grey-robed eminence.

Loric smiled. "It pleases me to serve my country. It pains me, however, to do what I must do next. My Lords, a great fraud has been perpetrated upon the kingdom. The woman on the dais is not the royal princess." Loric pointed at the peasants sitting next to Isolte, both of whom shrank at being singled out. "Those two are her parents. Indentured servants from Tarash. Untalents both."

Saroya stared at the woman next to Isolte. Now that Saroya knew what to look for, the woman obviously bore some relation to Martezha. The blonde straggly locks faded to grey, but the jade eyes, while worn down at the corners by life and all its cares, showed a clear resemblance. Martezha flushed a beet red, but Urdig's calm demeanor surprised Saroya.

"Are those the Baghore's?" he asked.

Loric frowned, disconcerted that Urdig knew their identities. "Yes, they admitted leaving a child by the name of Martezha Baghore at the Cloister."

"Then again, My Lord Dorn, it would seem that Veyle owes you yet another debt of gratitude for exposing this fraud. You may be sure we will punish the perpetrator." Urdig's face remained impassive but Saroya thought Loric looked nonplussed. Callor took Martezha by the hand and led her from the room. She did not look back at her true parents.

Loric spun and stabbed a finger towards Saroya. "Behold, the true daughter of Padvai of Roshan."

Saroya felt the room grow smaller.

Urdig yawned. "So you claimed the other night. My men have yet to uncover any proof."

"The ring she carries is not enough? The perfect mate to your wife's ring?" Saroya clutched the ring where it nestled against her throat. "The family resemblance is too great. No, you deny her because she is Untalented."

Eminence Daravela chimed in. "The Order has demanded more checks on Untalents for years. Now, the royal line is tainted! Do the Houses not wonder at the realm's affliction by sickness? It is a sign."

Shouts rang throughout the hall. Some nobles nodded in approval. Others appeared stunned. Saroya flinched at ugly comments aimed in her direction. Yet Urdig stayed composed.

Saroya stood up and cleared her throat. Several nobles jeered.

"There's just one flaw to Lord Dorn's argument," she said. "I'm not Urdig's daughter." Loric mouthed, *You're finished.* She pressed on. "I'm Dhilain's."

Loric looked as though he'd bitten into a rotten lemon. "That's impossible. The ring!"

Dhilain stepped in. "Yes. A puzzle ring. When all her children married, my mother gave a piece of the ring to each of us. One to Padvai, one to me." He looked Loric straight in the eye. "And one to Isolte." Isolte gaped at him in incomprehension. "I'm not a sentimental man. I gave my piece to the girl's mother."

Loric purpled. "The original ring Martezha stole was in Mistress Bardan's possession. Explain that away!"

Dhilain turned to Urdig. "Your Majesty, you have been the victim of a fraud, yes, but I say, the perpetrator of this fraud stands before you still." He pointed at Loric. "Who 'discovered' the existence of your supposed heir? Whose wife had access to Padvai's chambers and could have stolen the Roshan ring? Padvai might even have given it to Isolte as she lay dying, passing on a family heirloom. Little did she know the twisted purpose her sister would make of it. The whole thing's a setup."

Isolte shot up from her chair. "Lies! What lies are these, brother?" Saroya watched her face as she grasped at any straw. "Padvai told me herself! How else could we have stumbled across this particular girl? 'Our child.' The words came straight from her mouth."

Dhilain shrugged. "A child of House Roshan, yes. Padvai never approved of the way I treated my paramour. It weighed heavily on her conscience. No fault of mine you chose to misunderstand her." He continued. "You planted the first ring. But Loric's plan to embarrass and create scandal was foiled when a spiteful young women stole it."

"How dare you?" Loric asked. "I have always held the good of Veyle first and foremost. Isolte, tell them."

Isolte glanced at Loric then said, "I regret telling my husband about the child. I had no idea he would abuse my trust in this manner. I thought this a private family matter." She sat back down and ignored her husband.

Loric's eyes bulged. "You can't deny I have saved the city from the plague."

"Actually, I can," Callor replied. He turned to the door leading from the dais and motioned for the guard. Saroya watched Nalini, looking timid but determined, enter the hall. Nalini stepped forward and dropped a deep curtsy. Her hands trembled as they gripped her skirts.

"Are you the one who made this discovery?" Urdig asked as Nalini rose to her feet.

"No, Majesty." The master healer tried to cut her off.

Eminence Daravela directed a withering stare at Nalini. "In the name of the Order and your guild oaths, I command you to be silent."

"The Order holds no sway in the Hall of Nobles," Urdig said. "Please continue, Mistress Ferlen."

Nalini gulped, but lifted a shaking hand and pointed at Saroya. "This woman brought us the plant. She made the connection between the almshouse occupants' health, and the well. If it wasn't for her, we would still be searching for some way to stem the tide of fever."

Urdig winked at Saroya. "Is this true?"

She flushed bright red and for once didn't know what to say. Eiden Callor stepped forward. "My Lord, I can vouch for this story. Mistress Bardan took me to the almshouse in question, where we gathered the lichen. She insisted we bring it to the healers, and that they not know who delivered it."

"Whyever not?"

Saroya jumped in. "I'm in disfavour with the Healer's Guild. If they knew who brought them the plant, they'd ignore it."

Loric broke in, yelling now. "Unbelievable! This girl is Untalented. You would believe her over a titled lord of the Great Circle of Houses? And a childhood friend of hers over the master healer? The eminence?"

Nalini stood her ground. For once, her honesty worked to Saroya's advantage. "Captain Callor and I can both vouch for her."

Urdig faced the master healer. "Master Healer, do you deny the testimony?"

The master healer, after only a brief pause, stepped away from Loric and shook his head.

"Eminence Daravela?"

Daravela's lips thinned into a hard line. "This changes nothing. This monarchy is too soft on Untalents. The Order has the best interests of Veyle at heart." She omitted a curtsy as she exited the hall.

Nalini rushed up to Saroya and hugged her. Saroya kept her attention fixed on Urdig.

"Captain Callor, you will place Lord Dorn and his wife under house arrest at Manor Dorn until such time as any evidence of treason can be proven or not to the satisfaction of the Great Circle."

Callor grabbed Loric's arm. "No!" Loric yelled. "You can't do this!" Callor dragged Loric, still shouting, away. Saroya could not summon any emotion for him other than disdain. It was all he ever showed her, after all.

∞ ∾

Saroya and Nalini sat together in a corner of Urdig's study while they waited for the men to sort out with the healers how best to deploy resources distributing the cure.

"I haven't thanked you yet, Saroya."

"For what?"

"Mother was the first person I tested the water on. You saved her life." Nalini's voice shook.

Saroya hugged Nalini. All the tension in their friendship popped like a bubble when she released her. "Is she at least not giving you any more grief about being a healer?"

Nalini smiled. "I think they might be coming 'round."

"There's something I have to tell you," Saroya said. Overhearing, Eiden Callor cast her a warning glance. She shook her head. "I'm going to live at Manor Roshan."

"Really? Why? I thought ..."

"I ..." Saroya knew her friend would not appreciate being lied to. Her debt now to Urdig and Dhilain was binding, though. "It's all been a big misunderstanding." She said a silent goodbye to the mother she'd never known. "Queen Padvai wasn't my mother." Nalini gasped. "Apparently her brother, who I thought was my uncle, is my real father. He's head of House Roshan." She watched Nalini work out the trail of relationships in her head.

"But ... Really?"

Saroya nodded. If Nalini believed this story, all the rest would fall into place. Nalini looked back and forth between Saroya's copper locks and Dhilain's ginger hair. Then she smiled and hugged her again.

"And they've accepted you?"

Saroya couldn't summon her voice to answer. She nodded. Nalini's smile spread from ear to ear. She reached

out and wiped a tear from Saroya's cheek. She turned to face
the portrait of Queen Padvai that hung on the far wall.
"Your mother would be proud."

Saroya stared at her. "No, you don't understand ..."

"Oh, I think I do. Maybe one day when we're both old
and grey you can tell me all about it. Looks like the healers
are leaving. I'd better go—Master Healer Brinnig probably
has a few choice words for me. When you're settled, send me
a note." She squeezed Saroya's fingers and then rejoined the
knot of healers. Callor and Dhilain strode up to Saroya.

"She believed you?" Callor asked.

Saroya looked at them both. "If she didn't, she won't say
anything."

Dhilain smiled. "Come, you must be tired. I'll have
Guffin send over any possessions you might have. My wife is
eager to meet you."

Saroya didn't know what to say. No one had ever been
anxious to see her, ever.

CHAPTER 16

Saroya blinked as she raised her head off the fluffy down pillow. She listened to the soft patter of the rain on the cobbles in the courtyard. For an instant, she wasn't sure where she was then remembered her arrival the previous evening at Manor Roshan. Kasturi, Dhilain's wife, had folded her into her arms and shown her to her room—not a garret, but a suite in the family quarters.

She swung her legs onto the carpeted floor, stretched, and shrugged on a tunic. It might be raining but her heart felt sun warmed. She traipsed off to the kitchen in search of breakfast then went hunting for Dhilain. He had told her to find him after she had rested.

She located him in his study. In contrast to Loric's gloomy room, large windows overlooked the manor gardens, books lined the walls, and colourful tapestries offset plush furniture. Dhilain offered her a glass of lemon cider.

"Doesn't me being Untalented cause problems for you?"

Saroya asked.

"Do you feel Untalented?"

"The Adepts say so. But my Testing ..."

"Let me guess. Almost perfect?"

Saroya nodded. She blurted, "I think I know how to prevent the next plague, or at least stop it from spreading too far."

Dhilain smiled. "I don't doubt it."

"Really? Most people do doubt me."

"I'm not just humouring you, Saroya. There's a reason the Adepts want you to think you're Untalented." He settled back into his chair and steepled his fingers.

"Three hundred years ago, as today, one could be a Talent, or an Untalent, but also a third class of person—a Visionary. The last Roshan to sit on the throne of Veyle, King Pallen, was also the last Visionary who ruled.

"Visionaries were, and still are, what one could call multi-Talented. They might not know everything about any single Talent, but they know enough—in that field, and usually several others—to have insights that other people would not. They make connections and inferences that a Talent might overlook.

"I believe you are a Visionary. It's how you figured out the importance of that well, and probably why you have these ideas about the next plague."

"So I'm not Untalented."

"You might be, but I doubt it. True Untalents are extremely rare; almost everybody has at least one skill.

House Roshan has never produced a true Untalent, and Visionaries run in the family. Isolte and I are Talents, but Padvai was a Visionary herself."

"But why haven't I heard of Visionaries before?" Saroya caught herself as more and more questions came to mind.

Dhilain sighed. "Three hundred years ago, people respected Visionaries. Not that they're better than Talents, but they bring something different to the table. The noble Houses often chose a Visionary to lead the kingdom.

"Then the plague hit. People were dying in the streets. Factions jealous of Visionary power saw an opportunity— the guilds of Talent and the Adepts, and those noble Houses without Visionaries in their lines. The Order classified Visionaries as simple Untalents, and ostracized them. Pallen was assassinated. Our House was lucky to survive. We cultivated greedy Adepts and bribed them to certify our Visionaries as minor Talents. We toed the line—we'd lost too much to fight for our beliefs in the open."

"Why hide still? Three hundred years ..."

"The Adepts control Testing and the old histories are forgotten or rewritten. We bide our time. My father carefully selected Padvai's marriage—Urdig has a more open mind and we hoped she could sway him into an official softening of the laws. She just didn't have time."

Horror hit Saroya like a brick in the chest: how many of the Untalents she'd seen penned were also Visionaries? People just like her? People forced into captivity because they didn't conform to the Order's idea of Talent?

Dhilain gazed sadly out the window.

"So the only reason she hid me was because of Loric."

"She loved Loric once, but our father felt Urdig was the better match. When Urdig couldn't father a child, I think she chose with her heart and only afterwards realized her error."

"Loric hates me. Because I'm Untalented." *And because I remind him of what he could never have.*

"Some people can't see beyond what they've been told all their lives."

Dhilain looked at the ring at Saroya's throat. He lifted the leather thong over her head, undid the knot, and replaced the leather with a new gold chain.

"I still don't understand why she hid you from our House, but if I had to guess … Isolte would never forgive Padvai for her transgression with Loric, had she known."

Dhilain clasped the chain with its ring pendant around her neck.

"Why don't you explore the grounds and think on things for a bit. We can talk more later."

∞ ∽

The Manor Roshan grounds were smaller than Manor Dorn, but more intimate. A gravel path with flowering vines arching overhead led down to the canal promenade. Saroya strolled along the flagstones, not really seeing the barques floating by. She found herself at the stables, and reflected on how far she'd come since Durin offered her a position caring for the Cloister horses.

The clatter of hooves distracted her. To her surprise, Eiden Callor dismounted in the stable yard.

"What are you doing here?"

"Visiting my grandmother."

"I don't understand."

"Kimila. She's a servant here. Won't leave no matter how often I offer to pay for her own home. She says this is home."

Saroya remembered Kimila's long ago comment about some Untalents going far. Something clicked. "You're a Visionary too!"

Callor looked around, worried someone would overhear. He took her arm and led her into the garden.

"Does Urdig know?" Saroya asked.

"No. My grandmother raised me after brigands killed my parents. Airic of Roshan recognized me for what I was, and convinced me to throw my last Test in favour of one skill. I had enough military know-how for him to get me a posting with the cadets."

"And my mother?"

"A few years ago she became my patron." He shrugged. "It didn't hurt that I saved Urdig's life a few times on the battlefield."

Saroya stared at this man who'd been so maddeningly elusive ever since she'd met him in Adram Vale. Sometimes helpful, often angry. She saw him in a new light.

He stopped midstride and turned her to face him.

"I recognized something in you. Right from the start.

Something of myself. But I couldn't be sure, and I couldn't jeopardize Urdig. Not after all he and Padvai did for me."

She reached up and touched his cheek. "You did enough."

Eiden clasped her hand, shook his head. "I know too well what it's like to have to hide in plain sight." He bent, brushed his lips lightly against her forehead then walked up the path to the house. Saroya stared after him, trying to calm the sudden racing of her heart.

~ ~

Later, in the library, Dhilain offered Saroya a goblet of wine.

"My wife and I are childless. We discussed the matter and, with your permission, would like to adopt you as our own," Dhilain said.

Stunned, Saroya collected herself. A real family, after all this time—one that didn't think that she was Untalented, that didn't view the label as cause for shame.

Dhilain, seeming to understand her discomposure, changed the subject. "Tell me your thoughts on the plague."

Saroya explained to him how she'd collected so much data in tandem with her search for Veshwa. She spread out one of her maps of the Vergal on the table before her.

"These are the first places with plague, and the ones with the most cases." Saroya pointed at the port, and the granaries. "Rats thrive in all those places. And near refuse.

"I think the rats carry it and help its spread. It explains its presence in the port even though the first ship was quarantined—rats can get off via the mooring lines. The Vergal quarantine failed because there's no way to stop the rats from crossing the canals."

"You'll never get rid of all the rats."

"No. But …" Saroya told him about her ideas for ratproofing the granaries, and her scheme for an aqueduct system separate from the water supply to remove offal from the streets.

"You realize that outside this House, you are an Untalent. You'll have to shepherd these ideas along from the background."

"I understand." But she was already toying with the problem of Visionaries in general, and how to discredit the Order of Adepts. "But I know a receptive builder, and Urdig might help with official approval." She went on, outlining her plague-prevention solutions in detail.

Dhilain smiled and she looked into his interested, attentive eyes. Never again would she feel ashamed when someone sneered at her and called her Untalented. The word meant so much more to her now. Ideas whirled through her head and she no longer struggled to fit them into a single line of thought. It was enough to know that when she finally wove them into something greater, someone would be willing to listen.

ACKNOWLEDGEMENTS

A book doesn't get written without a lot of help. First and foremost, thanks to my husband, Guylain, for his love and support.

This book would have ended twenty-five pages in without Laisha Rosnau and her class on outlining. Lawrence Hill's Booming Ground Mentorship at UBC gave me the courage to continue. Thanks also to the SPIN writing group, Mary, June, and Jen for inviting me to readings and welcoming a genre writer into their midst.

A big thank you to kc dyer for pointing me to the KidCrit writing group, run by Marsha Skrypuch. Their feedback made the book much better, together with critiques by Hélène Boudreau, Helaine Becker, Carmen Wright, Sharon Jones, Valerie Sherrard, Darla Paskell, Reisa Stone, Shari M., Ashley, and Ivana.

Thanks also go to preliminary readers Tim Keating and Trish Loye Elliott.

Heather McDougal created the gorgeous cover, cleaned up my maps and put up with my nit picking.

For helping me to choose between cover designs, a big shout out to Karen, Sara and Julia Cauty, Colette Richardson and the young ladies at York House. Also Tenaya, Genevieve, Athena and Ruby, Hélène Boudreau, Patricia Bow, Stephen Geigen-Miller, Veronica Steiger-Gaboury, Sandra Wickham, Dan Wells, and Keffy Kerhli.

Saroya's adventures will continue in

VISIONARY

For more books by Ganache Media
visit
www.ganachemedia.com

Follow us on social media:

FB: www.facebook.com/ganachemedia
Twitter: @ganachemedia

Follow Katrina Archer online at

www.katrinaarcher.com

Social Media

FB: www.facebook.com/
katrinaarcherauthor

Twitter: @katrinaarcher

Katrina Archer lives and writes on her sailboat in
Vancouver, B.C., Canada, with a crew of husband, cat
and dog. Katrina knows all about being a dabbler,
having worked in aerospace, video games and film.

CPSIA information can be obtained at www.ICGtesting.com
Printed in the USA
LVOW07s0735021214

416526LV00001B/17/P